THE MOSAIC IV

A Compilation

of Short Stories

Edited by

Dr. Cassundra White-Elliott

CLF Publishing, LLC.
9161 Sierra Ave, Ste. 203C
Fontana, CA 92335
www.clfpublishing.org

Cover Design by Senir Design. Contact information-info@senirdesign.com.

ISBN # 978-1-945102-10-3

Printed in the United States of America.

Dedications

This book is dedicated to all aspiring writers who were told they couldn't make it in the field of writing or who may have been too scared to move forward because of a fear of failure.

The authors, whose stories are included within, are proof that you can be successful and your dreams can be a reality.

So, I invite you to pursue your own writing and be the success you know you are.

C. White-Elliott

Dr. Cassundra White-Elliott

Acknowledgements

I acknowledge all the participants in this project, who helped to see it from its stages of inception to its complete fruition.

May your success be plentiful, as you continue to pursue your educational and writing endeavors. I look forward to working with each of you individually, collectively, or both, in the near future.

Much love and appreciation,

C. White-Elliott

Dr. Cassundra White-Elliott

Table of Contents

Babysitting in the Suburbs

Krisha Mae Bacarro

"It doesn't matter who you are, or where you came from.
The ability to triumph begins with you, always."

Oprah Winfrey

On a chilly rainy afternoon, in the suburbs of Ohio, Maggie sat outside on her patio admiring the raindrops hitting every inch of the once steaming hot black concrete. Moving to Ohio just a couple months ago with nothing planned, it was a huge change for Maggie. She came from California, where there is no season other than a blazing hot summer. She used to live in a creepy old apartment complex. The walls were stained with filthy rust running in every corner of the apartment; the windows were so defective that every time a small car passed she called hear the windows rattle, and the floors were so ancient that the once smooth carpet had become almost as rough as sandpaper.

Maggie needed a new beginning, so she decided to move back to where it all started 28 years ago, in Ohio. She was almost as tall as your average football player with short dark brown hair, and her body looked as if she were active. Little did people know, Maggie never worked out in her life, except for when she was in that horrible place they made you go to when you were a kid. A bunch of grumpy old people, whiny little kids, and nothing but a wall built up around the place to keep you from being like a free bird that you once thought you were. At least that's what Maggie thought about elementary school.

Coming from an amazingly loving family, her grandparents decided to let her live in the home she grew up in. The interior of the house was just as beautiful as the breathtaking beauty of nature surrounding it. Going to Ohio, Maggie had no idea where to start when it came to looking for a job. Sure, she had hobbies she could put in use, but it didn't get her that far back in California. Luckily for her, her grandparents were really good friends with the next door neighbors. Tom and Carrie were such kind people. Tom is a 42-year-old goofy man, who worked as a lawyer, and Carrie is a 40-year-old loving woman, who worked at a correctional detention center for youth.

The beautiful couple had three kids of their own. Brett, the eldest, was tall for only being thirteen years old; Brandon, the middle child, was an awkward kid, but who isn't when they are only five years old just trying to find who they are in this enormous world they live in. then, there was Briana, the golden child, who was never in the wrong only because she was two years old. She sure was going through her terrible two's right then. The three kids sure did love their divine backyard. Because of how kid-like their backyard was, they never have the time to be inside playing on their now old dusty beat up PlayStation 3. Because Tom and Carrie had jobs that sometimes caused them to stay overtime or even go out to dinner for, they hired Maggie to be their full-time babysitter while she was on the lookout for a job.

As Maggie was daydreaming, she was interrupted by a buzzing sound that happened to be her phone. There it was, money waiting to be collected. It was Carrie on the other line.

"Hello?" Maggie answered.

"Hi, Maggie. It's Carrie! Tom and I were wondering if you're free tonight to watch the kids. Tom has a dinner with the firm, and well, we're planning on going if you're available?" Carrie asked with desperation in her voice.

"Of course! You know I am always thrilled to watch the munchkins!"

"Great! Thank you so much. See you tonight around 7:30?"

"See you then!"

Babysitting the kids was always a blast for Maggie. As she waited for the time to strike 7:30, she sat down to watch her favorite movie, *The Notebook.* That movie sure is a tearjerker. The beautifully directed movie has a love that Maggie longs for, an endless love.

At 7:30, Maggie arrived at the most elegant house she had ever encountered, the Fletcher's residence. She walked up the bright red brick steps and knocked on the smooth wooden front door. *Thump, thump, thump!* Maggie immediately knew the sound of those bear-like footsteps, the kids. She is then attacked by three little piranha-like kids.

"Kids, kids! Leave Maggie alone! Hi there, sweetie. You are such a life saver!" Carrie said, with a big smile on her face.

"It's really no big deal. I love the kids so much, as if they were my own siblings."

Tom and Carrie stood by the door looking ravishing as ever. Tom had on a navy blue suit that fit his body so well you can tell he had been working out lately, and Carrie with a sequined navy blue dress that brought out the color of her emerald-like eyes.

The two decided to leave right away because they would be late if they left any later. "Bye, kids. Be good for Maggie! Bye, Maggie. We should be back by midnight," Carrie said, as they walked out the door.

As soon as Tom and Carrie left, Maggie asked the kids if they were hungry. Of course, as growing kids, they were starving! She decided to make her oh so famous Chicken Alfredo. The kids loved it! From the soft well-seasoned chicken, to the slimy noodles that swirl everywhere. As the kids spent the rest of the night watching old Disney movies, Maggie cleaned up after them. When she finished the dishes, she went to the cozy living room where she joined the kids to watch *Beauty and the Beast*.

After Brandon and Briana fell asleep on the couch, Maggie gently carried them upstairs to their fairy-tale like bedrooms. Then, it was just Brett and Maggie watching *Dumbo*. In the middle of a scene, Maggie received a phone call from an artist that is well-known by her famous art studio. She was overly excited that she almost missed the call.

"Hello, Miss Lopez. I got your work from my assistant, and I reviewed it tonight. I would like to gladly inform you that it is with great pleasure to have you be a photographer here at my studio if you are still up for the job."

Trying hard not to wake the kids, Maggie replied, "OH YES! Mrs. Jenny. Thank you so much. It is MY great pleasure to accept the job!"

Maggie hung up the phone after talking for twenty minutes and jumped with excitement. She had been awaiting the call ever since she sent in her work seven months ago. She couldn't wait to celebrate by herself with a glass of cold refreshing white wine.

Eleven o'clock rolled around, and in came Tom and Carrie. They came home to find all the kids sound asleep upstairs and Maggie looking like she just won a million dollars. Maggie informed the couple about the job opportunity. After a long thoughtful conversation, they came to an agreement that Maggie would still continue to work for them when she was available, and everything would stay the same. So, both parties were happy.

About the Author

Krisha Mae W. Bacarro is a young caring girl, originally from Charleston, South Carolina. She currently resides in Highland, California with her mother, little brother, and her older brother. Krisha Mae is a massive fan of romantic-dramas, but steered away from that genre when writing. Her favorite author happens to be the American novelist, screenwriter, and producer, Nicholas Sparks. She hopes to pursue a nursing career and eventually work with kids in the near future. Krisha Mae might act like a goofball at times, but when it's time for business, she knows how to buckle down and get serious.

The Walk

Parker Balders

"There is no honorable way to kill, no gentle way to destroy.
There is nothing good in war except its ending."

Abraham Lincoln

One day, I walked down an unknown path where the trees talked and shadows walked. There was no one in sight, for the trees were walls to keep me from humanity. The trees stood tall, almost as if they never ended. The sun was not found in this forest, because the leaves and branches above shielded the barrage of sunrays pouring down on top of me. The forest was completely mute of all sounds. When I stepped on a branch, it rang through the forest like a gunshot. That one second of disturbance felt like I was dishonoring the silent woods.

The trees are wrapped in moss and had thick roots. The roots acted as bear traps, just waiting for me to trip over them. There were leafs that were scattered on floor, waiting to be broken by unwatching feet. The branches covered what was the sky, by creating their own.

Time in the forest was completely still. It felt, as I walked, that time was lost and was trying to find me. It felt like that for everything else as well as noises, thirst, hunger, and even animals. In this forest, only the trees can find you, nothing else.

As I walked, a sound broke out from the distance. A sound unfamiliar to the forest, where no sound is found. It rang from tree to tree. I stood there, curious of what lay there so far away. A sound I recognized, but was lost in my memories. No matter how hard I searched through them. I walked towards the far away noise. I saw lights in the distance and heard weird noises coming from there. As I approached, I saw another human.

He was surrounded by a bright, spontaneous fire, with a piece of metal grasped between his lips. He wore a long leather jacket, with jeans, and a white undershirt. He had a beard, and a hat that was round and torn. He was rough and dirty. He had a voice that was scratchy and deep. He looked no older than 40.

I looked curiously at the metal he had. He asked, "Haven't you seen a harmonica before?" I thought long and hard trying to find the answer in my head. He said, "It doesn't matter." He looked down at the harmonica and said, "I know why you're here." I didn't even know why I was there. He looked up at me and then said, "Take a seat." He gestured to a big stone that was on the other side of the fire. He then said, "You suffered an unfortunate fate, haven't you kid?"

I didn't know what he was talking about. He said, "As you walk you get more and more lost, but yet you are finding your way back." His words were unclear and mysterious, but they still made sense to me. I don't know why they did. He sighed and said, "Soon, I will help you find your way through these woods, but first let me play for you my harmonica." He played a tone that was peaceful and warm. It echoed through the forest bringing it to life. The fire kept me warm and comfortable. It was as if I was being held by a beautiful woman. Her name is Sandra... "Who's Sandra?" I asked myself, as I slowly slipped into the night.

I woke up cold and alone. I looked around my area, only to find no remnant of the man or the fire he had created the night before. Only the rocks we sat on were there. The forest was different that day. The sun finally found its way through the leaves and branches that were keeping it out. It brightened the forest around me, showing its true face. There was only one unordinary thing in this forest. Everywhere I walked, there was a painted red trail that followed. I kept walking deeper into the forest and also in my mind. I asked questions to myself like, "Who was that man?" and "How did I get lost in the first place?" and finally, "Who is Sandra?" I walked until darkness once again covered the forest around me.

I found myself getting weaker, and it wasn't because I was hungry. It was a slow weird sensation that was slowly eating away at me. The forest was cold that night, and it kept getting colder. I walked until I was finally drained of all my energy. I was falling asleep, while trying to keep my eyes open. Then, the silence was pierced by the loudest bang I have ever heard through my ears. It sounded like a tree was chopped down and shook the world it landed on. I stood up and walked toward the noise.

More and more extremely loud noises protruded from the thick beyond. I fell down, and I was too weak to stand up. It felt like my body rejected my legs. My body was growing colder. I crawled until I could see an open field, where I saw something astonishing. There was a huge battle taking place between two sides.

By that point, I remembered everything. I looked at my attire. I was dressed in a full blue uniform. I noticed something off. A red mark left on my chest. I touched it and noticed it was blood, leaving my body. I sat there holding onto my life like a child about to fall off a wagon. I was dying. I looked at a tree with a sign posted. It read, "Gettysburg." I let go of the pressure I was applying to my wound and looked up towards the leaves above. I was falling in and out of consciousness.

The last thing I remember was my wife Sandra. She looked at me, smiled, and then kissed me goodnight.

About the Author

Parker Balders was born and raised in Crestline, California. He has two siblings and parents that appreciate him. All his family and friends are the people that keep him pushing for his dreams. He enjoys writing and creatively thinking outside the box. He wrote this short story as a tribute to the people who fought for our freedom. To him, his freedom is everything, and with it, he was able to write this story.

Gone Too Soon:

A Friendship Tested

Ruben Baltierra

"Every new day is another chance to change your life."

Ruben Baltierra

Anthony, a regular high school boy, who was sixteen, had two best friends: Brandon and Jake. They had been best friends since the sixth grade, and they were all so lucky to have met each other. Anthony was more close to Brandon than Jake, due to Brandon being sillier and outgoing. Brandon is somebody you can call on and will be there in a flash, as well as somebody who is reliable and there when you need him. On the other hand, Jake was quieter and more reserved than Brandon.

At school, Anthony had possibly the biggest crush on a girl named Selena, who just so happened to sit behind him in class. Selena was for sure a beauty. Her hair was a rich shade of mahogany. It flowed in waves to adorn her glowing, porcelain-like skin. Her eyes, framed by long lashes, were a bright, emerald green and seemed to brighten the world. With a straight nose and full lips, she seemed like the picture of perfection. Had she smiled, the world would sigh with contentment. Had she laughed, the world would laugh with her. And had she cried, the whole world would want to comfort her. He would get nervous every time he spoke in front of the class due to her presence. To top it all off, she had had a crush on him since eighth grade, with his best friends Brandon and Jake knowing. Nevertheless, she never once tried to speak with him because she couldn't speak or even breathe when he was near her, so she tried to save the embarrassment.

One day on a dark and stormy night, a friendship became tested when Anthony knew Jake had a crush on Selena, his best friend out of all people. That night, Jake went to Anthony's house just to make sure Anthony was fine.

"I would never intentionally hurt you. You know that," Jake said.

"I know. It's just that I can't believe all this. She knew that I liked her, but how come she..," he started to cry.

"She's not the only one. You can get a better girl than her," he told Anthony.

It was real hard for Anthony to handle all the information he had found out, so he called Brandon for guidance. Brandon knew how to handle all these things because he had been dating girls since eighth grade. That was no shocker to Anthony due to Brandon being very handsome and kind.

A week later, Anthony was busy setting everything up for his birthday party. He was planning on a big extravagant party that would consist of many different activities including paintball, live music, ultraviolet lighting and smoke machines, and bunch of free food and drinks. That evening, Jake went to his house with none other than, Selena.

"It's not what you think," Jake said.

"It's nothing. I'm over her," Anthony replied back, sounding like he didn't care, but in reality he did. He gave her a smile and went to his room wanting to scream and shout out loud. He was constantly thinking over why his best friend would do that to him and how Jake told him he would never break his heart. That night, Anthony tried his best to enjoy his party, while avoiding Selena and Jake for the rest of the night.

The next day, Anthony didn't bother going to school. He just lay in bed all day long thinking about what would happen to his friendship. He thought over and over about how he felt betrayed by Jake because he felt he could trust Jake all his life, but in the back of Anthony's mind was that he would rather lose everything as long as Jake was fine. Anthony kept growing weaker due to not eating a thing since the night before. He decided not to go to school for a few days. He told his mother that he wanted to go to his village for a few days to relax. She totally supported him since she knew that every time Anthony had a serious problem he'd go to his village. His village was located approximately 60 miles away from his house and had a peaceful scenery. The place was filled with an abundance of flowers, a small pond, and hut.

One day, without even thinking anything bad would happen, a tall, very masculine guy came and sat next to him. It was Jake.

He said, "Why are you avoiding me? Don't tell me that this is all about that girl," Jake said.

Anthony stood up seemingly mad and said, "No. Just leave me alone!" Anthony's shout caused the whole school to look interested.

"What are you doing? Running away from me? For all these years and all we've been through? How could a girl ruin our friendship? You can't just run away from me. You know that. Stop acting like a fool! Please! I need my friend back. I really wanted to see you and to tell you something," Jake said passionately.

Anthony was in a loss of words, but it only angered him more. "You want to tell me something? Why don't you go tell something to Selena? I'm no longer your friend. I never thought you could do this to me. Why on Earth did you come with her to my birthday party? It's not a joke! You promised that you would never hurt me. I guess you tend to break promises. I should never have trusted you all these years. I should have trusted what people said about you!" Anthony shouted and went away.

Jake was in a world of confusion and in a state of shock. He couldn't understand what he had done, but felt he wasn't the one at fault. But, it was Anthony. The next day at school, Brandon told Anthony that Jake moved to Miami with his mother.

Two years later, Anthony, as well as Brandon, graduated with honors. Anthony continued his studies in Miami, to be able to reconcile his differences with Jake again, and Brandon decided to travel the world first. Then one day, at the local market on the small downtown strip on South beach, he saw Jake's mother.

"Aunt Reese, how are you? Where's Jake?" he asked.

Aunt Reese smiled and then shed a tear unexpectedly and said, "Would you mind having dinner with me? There's something I want to give you."

Anthony happily accepted with joy. Jake's house was big and lovely, with lots of flowers that included roses to lilies. Having dinner without Jake, Anthony was wondering where he was. After dinner, Aunt Reese gave him an envelope.

"This is it. Open it. Read it when you go home. It's from him," Aunt Reese told Anthony, which left him in a confused state of mind.

Anthony went home and quickly opened the envelope. The letter said, "Hi there, Anthony. First of all, I want you to know that I miss you. I hope you miss me, too. I know you are wondering why I wrote this letter. When you read this letter, I'm no longer here anymore. Remember, the last day we saw each other? I wanted to tell you something. I was sick due to having a brain tumor. Yes. I suffered from a brain tumor, and I really wanted to tell you. It's just that, I had no idea how. I really hope you can forgive me. I want you to know too, that I came to the party with Selena because she wanted to tell you that she likes you. I was surprised too when she told me that. She was just saying that I like her because she wanted to know whether you really liked her or not. So, now you know. I forgive you. And, I hope you can forgive me, too. Please. Anthony, I know. See me in heaven. P.S. Forever, you're my best friend. Don't blame yourself. It's not your fault."

Suddenly, tears were running down Anthony's cheeks. He felt he made a big mistake. He went to see Aunt Reese to hug her, "Remember, dear. Don't you ever blame yourself," Aunt Reese gave him a smile. Anthony couldn't believe that Jake was no longer there anymore. "Life must go on. I will always remember him and keep him in my heart forever."

About the Author

Ruben Baltierra was born on August 17, 1997, in Mesa, AZ. Since 2011, Ruben has lived in San Bernardino, CA, where he graduated from Citrus Valley High School in 2015. Now, Ruben is attending Crafton Hills College, where he is studying to become a Radiologist. Ruben's hobbies are listening and playing music, writing, drawing, and occasionally playing sports.

The Escape

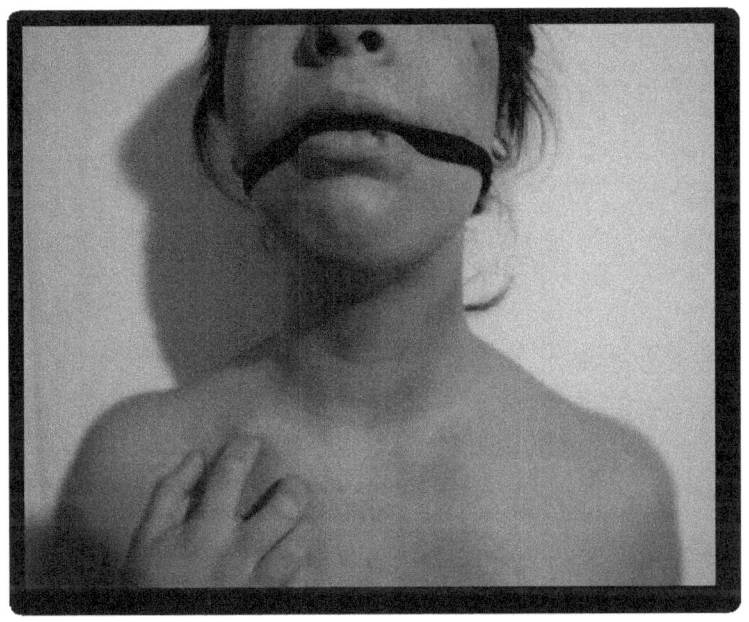

Patricia Carrasco

"We'd stare into the face of death, and death blinked first.
You'd think that would make us feel brave and invincible.
It didn't."

Rick Yancey

Alison Reese was the most beautiful girl at Lake Washington High. She was eighteen years old, 5' 6", had long shiny black hair, big blue eyes, and the warmest smile anyone had ever seen. Alison was very well known, not just by everyone in school, but also everyone in her community. She was loved for her cheerful and spunky attitude. She was able to put a smile upon anyone's face. Alison had a very bright future ahead of her; she was valedictorian of her senior class and was also receiving not one, but two scholarships for tennis and softball. That was until she was kidnapped on May 10, 1998.

Alison's mother asked if she would drive downtown to the grocery store to pick up a pot roast and wine, because they would be expecting guests for dinner. It was a gloomy Sunday afternoon, and the Washington air smelled of rain. That told Alison the streets would be empty, as the folks in her town would be indoors avoiding the rain. Alison never really enjoyed going to the grocery store. Men always tried flirting with her there, as if that was a place to pick up women. But none of them made her more uncomfortable than the butcher. People knew him as Mr. Morris. He always stared at Alison but never approached her. He watched her from the moment she walked in, until the time she walked out the door. He was a heavy man, weighing roughly two hundred and fifty pounds. He was bald and wore outdated glasses that looked like they were from the 70's era. As Alison shopped, she could feel his eyes on her, following her every move. Alison tried to pretend she didn't notice. She then paid for her items and causally walked out of the store, trying not to draw attention to herself.

On Alison's way home, she realized she had forgotten the bottle of wine her mother had asked for. She decided to head back to the store. When Alison walked in, she noticed that Mr. Morris wasn't at his station. That made Alison feel at ease. She paid for the wine then hurried back to her car, not wanting to worry her mother.

As she was entering her car, she felt an odd presence behind her and smelled the scent of blood. Suddenly, everything went black. When Alison came to, she wasn't sure where the hell she was. Her heart was racing, and her head was pounding. She felt something wet running down her neck. It was her blood. She then realized she was in a moving vehicle. Alison was unable to make out her location, as she was very disoriented, but she was able to make out the man driving. It was Mr. Morris. He was breathing very heavily and was covered in sweat.

The car then came to a sudden stop. He then opened the car door and threw Alison over his shoulders, carrying her into a cabin deep in the Washington forest. Alison began to scream and started fidgeting. Mr. Morris gave her a blow to the face, causing a fracture her left cheek. Tears ran down her face, but what Alison didn't know was that her nightmare had only begun. When Alison never returned home, her mother became extremely worried. Soon, police were scattered out everywhere looking for her.

Days turned to months, and months turned to years. Years of mental, physical, and sexual abuse. Alison gave up any hope of ever being found again. Soon, she became pregnant. On March 20, 2000, she gave birth to her son Jason. Alison didn't see her capturer in Jason. She only saw her beautiful child, and she swore to love and protect him at all cost. Once Jason turned five, he still had not seen the world outside the cabin. Alison kept the outside world a secret from Jason, not knowing if they would ever be free and to prevent him from asking any questions as to why they were unable to leave. She tried to keep the cabin as nurturing and normal as she could for Jason's sake.

The abuse didn't end there. Anytime Mr. Morris abused Alison, she would tell Jason to hide in the closet and not to come out until she gave the 'okay.' Soon, Alison became extremely sick with Cancer. Unable to get out of bed, Alison knew what her future held. Later that night, she died. Jason cried and screamed when he discovered his mother's body. Mr. Morris grabbed Jason by the hair and threw him into the closet. He then wrapped Allison in a blanket and took her lifeless body away.

Jason lay and wept in the closet for hours. Once Jason was able to calm himself down, he crawled out of the closet and lay where Alison's body once was. Mr. Morris had still not returned. As Jason rested, he put his hand under Alison's pillow noticing something under it. It was a list. A list of very precise directions. 1) Stay hidden 2) Keep quiet 3) When Mr. Morris goes upstairs, run out the door. 4) Don't stop running, and 5) Find someone and ask for help. As scared as Jason was, he was afraid of Mr. Morris a lot more. So, Jason did exactly what his mother had asked. When Mr. Morris arrived, scared Jason waited, then ran straight for the door. Once outside, he was so amazed by the trees, the blue sky, and the way the dirt felt beneath his feet. But, he didn't stop running. He found the road where he noticed a couple walking their dog. Three days later, Mr. Morris was found and arrested.

About the Author

Patricia Carrasco is an 18-year-old college student, born in Rancho Mirage, CA. She is currently studying at College of the Desert Community College, in Palm Desert. Patricia graduated from Indio High School, in June of 2016. While at College of the Desert, she plans to obtain her associates degree. She then plans to transfer to the University of California, at Riverside in the fall of 2018, where she will major in biology. At Indio High School, Patricia was involved in The Future Farmers of America program where she raised a pig and sold him at the National Date Festival in Indio, California. In the future, Patricia aspires to become a zoologist and travel the world, so she may help and protect wildlife.

Daniel and the Craziest Welcome Home Party in History

https://www.dieepic.com

J.D. Delgado

"Keep your dreams alive. Understand to achieve anything requires faith and belief in yourself, vision, hard work, determination, and dedication. Remember, all things are possible for those who believe."

Gail Devers

It was a sunny and oven-like Monday morning. Daniel Blaze had no idea what to do. He was thinking about whether or not he really wanted to get out of bed that morning. "Screw it," he said to himself. He lifted himself from his bed. He was drenched in sweat, as if someone had poured water on his back. He could not sleep the night before because he couldn't stop thinking of his son Peter. He woke up with a sore neck. He must've had a violent nightmare because his bed sheets and pillows were all over his floor, as if he had thrown them from his bed.

Every day, he wished he could have his son back. But, there was no bringing him back from the dead. Daniel hated himself for not being there when his son had died. He also wished he had been there for his birthday. Daniel was stationed in Afghanistan with the U.S. Army as a Staff Sergeant. Daniel couldn't believe that he couldn't be home for the birth of his son; let alone the tragic death of his son. His son as far as he knew was seven years old and died of sudden unexpected death syndrome. When Daniel's son died, Jenna his wife of fifteen years had left him because she couldn't stand having to deal with the death of her firstborn without her husband there by her side.

When Daniel received the divorce papers, he couldn't believe it. The woman he loved was deciding to leave him. He didn't know how to handle it because she was his first love. Daniel decided that he would try to write her a letter, try to make amends, and try to convince her to stay with him. Months went by after Daniel sent the letter, and finally, he received a response from Jenna. The letter said:

> Dear Daniel,
>
> I appreciate your love and caring words. I don't think that I can be with you if you are in the army. Unless you are here, I don't want to live a life where I am always wondering when you are going to come home. I have been going through a depression since Peter died weeks after you had to go back to base. If you love me, please come home.
>
> Sincerely,
>
> *Jenna*

Daniel had thought about the letter for a while. Daniel didn't know what to say. He decided he would ask his brothers in the army. His buddy Sev had said to add Handsome Manboy on Snapchat. Daniel asked why he should follow Shauniee Stylez. Sev looked at Daniel like he was crazy. Sev then replied, "Shauniee always has beautiful girls, funny stories, and great tips once in a while. He even invented the best coffee concoction ever!" Sev kept rambling on and on about Shauniee. Daniel figured he would just add Shauniee on Snapchat. Daniel waited some time and finally got his add-back on snapchat and decided to tell Shauniee about his situation. Daniel watched his story after his duties on the base were done.

Shauniee appreciated that someone in the military had contacted him for advice. Off the bat, Daniel could tell Shauniee was a down-to-earth and kind-hearted person because the first thing Shauniee said was to fight for Jenna and to make sure those fifteen years of marriage were not a lie or a waste of time. Daniel decided he would contact the Sergeant Major of the Army. He told the Sergeant Major he would like to make arrangements to have a leave of absence from the army to mend situations back home. Sergeant Major looked at Daniel and thought about it for a few minutes and then decided to grant the leave of absence. Daniel was so grateful for the Major's decision and waited to board the plane with other soldiers who were going home.

On the way back to California, Daniel pondered what he would say to Jenna. It had been years since he had left for Afghanistan. It would be about a twenty-five-hour flight back to California, so Daniel figured he might as well get comfortable and think of what he was going to tell Jenna. He hadn't seen her in so long, and he didn't know what to expect when he saw her. He decided he would just rest, take a nap, and either let his dreams give him an idea of what to do. Daniel also thought about winging it and just letting her know on the spot how he felt and what he wanted out of their relationship. As his mind kept racing, his eyes became heavier and heavier. Soon, he found himself asleep on the plane.

His dream felt so real. He was still in his seat on the plane, but something was wrong. All the soldiers who were on the plane with him were not there. No seat was filled and it was too quiet. Daniel decided to investigate the plane's cabin. Both floors of the plane were empty. Daniel thought that was very odd. He decided to try and gain access to the cockpit, but there was something odd about the cockpit entrance. There was blood oozing from under the door.

As soon as Daniel pulled the door as hard as he could, he was horrified. The pilot and copilot were indeed in the plane, but they were zombies. As soon as Daniel made his way in and realized what happened, the copilot zombie had turned around and let out a groan. That caused chills to go down Daniel's spine and the hairs on the back of his neck stand up. As soon as Daniel turned around, he was faced with all the soldiers and flight attendants as zombies. Daniel was frozen. There was nowhere to go. Soon all the zombies had surrounded him and started to bite him. At that moment, Daniel screamed in pain. One of the zombies shook his arm. Again it shook his arm.

Then, the zombie started to talk and said, "Staff Sergeant Blaze!" Daniel looked at the zombie confused. How could this zombie talk?

Again, the Zombie shook Daniel and yelled, "STAFF SERGEANT BLAZE, WAKE UP!" At that moment the dream went dark. Daniel opened his eyes to his fellow soldiers surrounding him.

One of the soldiers said, "That must've been one hell of a nightmare, Serge."

"You have no idea," Daniel replied.

"Well now that that's over, you can get the hell off the plane. We landed in LAX about a half hour ago. I think you're the only one left that has family still waiting."

Daniel exited the plane and proceeded to the baggage claim. While waiting for his bags, Daniel heard a woman's voice behind him say, "You bastard! I thought you weren't going to come back home." Daniel simply smirked when he heard this. He remembered that voice. He turned around to meet his wife.

She had not changed much in the seven years he had been away. She was a tall cardinal-red haired woman with hypnotizing crystal clear blue eyes and a beautifully copper toned body. She was like an angel. He hugged her, and the two shared a tearful and passionate kiss. The two could not believe that that was actually happening. Once they finally were able to collect themselves, they picked up Daniel's bags and headed to the car. Daniel hadn't spoken a word since he got off the plane.

He decided to break the silence and jokingly said, "Jeez baby, you could have warned me that you were coming, I almost thought I was either going to have to stay at the airport overnight or arrange for an Uber to pick me up."

Jenna laughed and said, "You really think that I am going go another minute without seeing you?" Daniel smiled. He didn't want to go another minute without seeing her either.

It was a long drive home. It was weird though because instead of driving to their house in Anaheim, they were headed to Irvine. Daniel was confused and anxious. He decided that he would ask Jenna why they were going to Irvine. All of the sudden, she had a sad and serious face.

"I couldn't stay in that house anymore, not after…" Jenna paused and pulled over to wipe tears from her eyes. Daniel understood then what happened but let Jenna continue. "…So after that happened, I sold the house and remembered how you and your mom would always talk about moving back to Irvine, the quiet and safe neighborhood. I found a house with three floors. It has an attic and a basement. I took care of all your stuff to make sure it was clean before you came back and messed it up…"

Daniel laughed because he knew he would make himself right at home and make a mess to make sure he knew where everything was. Jenna playfully socked him and continued, "…and there is one final thing you're going to love. There is someone really anxious to meet you." Daniel was confused. Besides going to see his mother who else in town here is excited to see him?

The two finally arrived at the house. Something was strange though. He heard yelping like a tiny dog barking from inside the house. Right after he heard that, his heart beat like it hadn't before. Suddenly and immediately, his confusion turned into excitement. Jenna led Daniel into the house to the room where the source of the barking was coming from. There at their feet behind a baby gate stood a small German Shepherd-Siberian husky puppy. It was as small as a Chihuahua with a lot of fluff. Its coat was all black, except for the white-boot-like paws and middle section of its stomach. The strange trait that Daniel noticed was that one eye was sky blue and the other an emerald-green color.

"His name is Balto. I wanted to keep him a surprise until you got here. Besides, I can tell he already likes his dad because you're the first person to see him that he didn't start barking at."

Daniel walked closer to Balto. The puppy tried to stand up and lean on the fence but was too small to reach the top. Daniel reached in with both hands to pick Balto up. He could not believe that Jenna had done that all for him. It's almost as if all his dreams were coming true.

As it turned out, all his time for his service in the army was what made the dream possible. Because he was a high ranking officer, it helped pay for the house. Later Jenna admitted that her saying that she wanted to break up with him was all a ploy to get him back to California. She also said she wasn't alone. She had help from the sergeant major, Sev, and Shauniee Stylez himself.

At first Daniel was angry, but then he couldn't help but appreciate what Jenna had done. He even found himself laughing because he figured that he probably would have done the same thing. Jenna's plan was one that took a while to actually formulate. Sergeant Major had received a letter from Jenna months before she mentioned anything about a divorce to Daniel. She let the Sergeant Major know her situation. First, he had said it would be difficult for leave and that he would try to work something out. After that letter, another followed for Jenna stating Daniel's leave would be allowed once he asked for it.

That was where Jenna's plan hit a rocky take off. Jenna then remembered Daniel's old buddy Sev. She thought of how she would contact him. She decided to just play it by ear. She asked herself how many Sev's would there be in the army? Of course, with her luck, it turned out that he was the only Sev in the army. She asked him to try and convince Daniel to come back home and give him advice about contacting Shauniee Stylez to see what he would say. Of course, the man that stated he was "The Best to Ever Do It" truly lived up to his word. His advice eventually influenced Daniel's decision and convinced him to talk to the Sergeant Major. As Jenna finished explaining her "chain of messages," Daniel became more impressed than he had ever been with Jenna. He didn't think that her plan seemed easy to execute.

Daniel took time out of his day, and while spending quality time with Balto and Jenna, he wrote letters of thanks to Sergeant Major and Sev. Major said that Daniel could come back whenever he wanted, just say the word and he'd be welcomed back on base with an open door and open arms. Sev wrote him back saying "No problem, bro. Just be safe. Don't finish celebrating just yet, because I will be there soon as well to really get the celebration going." Daniel was ecstatic to read that.

Life was coming together. He then remembered Shauniee Stylez's thank you and decided to get on snapchat and personally thank the man himself for the little plan. Shauniee humbly replied to him saying, "Thank you again for your service in the army! I am glad that I was able to help out one of my Manboy Mafia Members." Daniel then thought to himself about it for a second... *That's it!* He'll invite Shauniee over, so that the welcoming home party for him and Sev would be perfect. With Shauniee, Daniel knew that he would take the party to the next level.

The next morning was perfect because it happened to be "Take off Tuesday," which was Shauniee's day off where he would occasionally answer snaps. Of course, Daniel again got the attention of Shauniee at the most opportunistic time, and of course, Shauniee replied right away as if to greet an old friend. Daniel could not keep his excitement in any longer and yelled, "Woohoo!!" That made Balto howl for the first time. The scene made Jenna giggle and record the ordeal to send it to Shauniee to bring more attention to the trio. Both Daniel and Jenna sent a message to Shauniee saying that his dog Stylez was more than welcome to come with him. This made Shauniee happy because he hated leaving Stylez at home. So everything was set. The party was just days away. Sev's flight was coming in that night, and Shauniee's flight was coming the next morning.

Daniel allowed the guys to unpack completely and get comfortable. Stylez and Balto got along very well. Stylez was laid back, and Balto was a little ball of fluff, playfully nipping at Stylez. Days went by, until finally the day of the party had arrived. That was the day when people would get crazy! Sure enough, word got out somehow that Shauniee Stylez was in California and the people that showed up knew exactly where to go. Over five hundred people ended up at the party!

At first Daniel, Jenna, and Sev were worried everything would go wrong. But, everything went fine… until it struck midnight.

The moon began to change into a burgundy red, and people began fighting each other. Daniel, Shauniee, Sev, and Jenna looked at each other in horror.

"What the hell is going on?" Sev and Daniel wondered. Shauniee and Jenna seemed to know what was going on.

"Follow me," Jenna said hurriedly. The three guys followed Jenna into the basement. Daniel had not checked out the basement. It was almost like a tunnel-like cave that went on for miles. They came to a door that had a huge sticker with "Die Epic" (Shauniee smirked and shook his head at that.) and a thumbprint scanner that only opened with Jenna or Daniel's. When Jenna opened the door, there were weapons, armor, and vehicles of various kinds. Daniel and Sev were impressed. They saw some shit in the army, but that took the cake. When the four gathered their weapons, they went back up to the chaos ensuing the house and neighborhood. They all looked to Shauniee, and he was startled for a second and said, "If we're going to die, it might as well be epic!"

They fought to the death, yet the violent crowds kept coming! They decided to attempt to use one of the vehicles that resembled the X-Jet from X-Men, in the basement and flew it up to the moon to see what was going on. An evil dictator by the name of Ryan Pain had a machine that caused the moon to turn red make people on earth angry and violent all the time. Shauniee and Jenna attempted to distract Pain with success. Daniel and Sev were able to disable the machine. Then, came the difficult task at hand, and that was to take out Pain. They had guns that when they fired upon Pain, he instantly went down. Everyone breathed a sigh of relief. The moon started to turn back to its normal white color. The gang packed up all the machinery, weapons and Pain himself into the jet. They headed home back to earth to see if everything was back to normal.

At first they were a bit skeptical about whether or not the town was back to normal. As soon as they exited the basement to the backyard of the house, the five hundred people that were at the party were still there as if nothing had happened. One of the party goers even said, "Hey I found them!" Apparently, the party goers weren't aware of the whole situation, but they somehow remembered that the four of them had slipped away for quite some time. The party continued, and one party goer pulled a string and a white neon sign lit up that said, "DIE EPIC." The party went on until the next day. Then, everyone had to go home because the next day was Monday, or in other words, back to work or for those who had the day off "Manboy Monday!" Shauniee told everyone to get home safe. As soon as everyone was gone, it was Daniel, Jenna, Sev, and Shauniee again.

Sev spoke up and said, "Well, that was one hell of a welcome back, Jenna." The guys all looked at Jenna.

"Well, I didn't expect all that to happen," Jenna said smiling.

Sev said, "Well I'm going back to base tomorrow, so Afghanistan will seem like nothing. Thanks again for having me."

"It wouldn't have been a party without you, brother," Daniel said.

Shauniee then spoke up, "Well, guys. It's time for me and Stylez to leave."

Daniel said, "Don't worry, bro. I'll take you and Sev to the airport."

Off the three guys and Stylez went to the airport. Jenna waved goodbye to Sev and Shauniee with Balto in her arms. When the trio arrived at the airport, Daniel unloaded all the bags for Shauniee and Sev. Sev's flight was the first to go, but before he left, he hugged Shauniee who gave him a Die Epic sticker. Daniel gave Sev a medallion with a yin and yang symbol, but instead of circles, it had wolf paws on the inside of both halves. That helped him get through rough times by just repeating, "Everything gets better in the end."

Shauniee's flight to New Jersey was up next. First, Daniel gave Stylez a pat and said, "Be a good boy!"

Then Daniel turned to Shauniee and said, "Thank you for everything you've done man. You are truly the best to ever do it."

Daniel gave Shauniee a hug and in return Shauniee gave Daniel an exclusive Die Epic t-shirt that was in army UCP colors. Daniel said it was the greatest shirt that he'd ever seen. Daniel left Shauniee at the terminal and started driving home.

For the next few years, Jenna and Daniel became closer. Daniel decided he would take a backseat on going back to the army and start his family life again with Jenna. Sev ended up becoming a Sergeant Major. Shauniee ended up getting a lot of media attention from his snapchat that he actually ended up making and staring in his own movie.

About the Author

J.D. Delgado is an author who loves writing stories that tickle the minds of readers. He was born in Orange, CA, but spent most of his life in Anaheim and Fullerton. J.D., as a child, was a great writer and speller. In 2015, he decided to pursue his passion for writing. In 2016, J.D. decided to use his dreams and nightmares as inspiration for his stories. He aspires to be on the list of greatest authors ever known.

The Pearl

Alicia Diaz

"In the end, you should always do the right thing even when it's hard."

Nicholas Spark

Adella had always been a curious mermaid. Her favorite thing to do was explore the ocean for new treasures. Most of the items that Adella found were human objects, such as combs, jewelry, glasses, wallets, money, and many other items. Adella was the only mermaid who enjoyed doing this because she was not aware that these items were just lost, invaluable items. She truly believed they were treasures.

One day, Adella was doing her daily "treasure hunt," and she stubbed her scaly, emerald green tail on an oyster. After saying a few curse words under her breath, she picked up the shell and opened it to find an alluring, luminescent, white pearl. This pearl was not like an ordinary pearl. This pearl had a glow to it that made it extremely obvious that it was an actual treasure. Once Adella was done being awestruck by this pearl, she put it back inside its shell, closed it back up, and stuffed it in her special treasure bag. As she was making her journey back home, Adella could not stop smiling from ear to ear. All she could think about was sharing her new treasure with everyone back home.

When Adella finally made it back to her house, she swam straight to her mom to share the special oyster with her. As soon as her mom saw the shell, her eyes widened and her mouth dropped. Adella's mother immediately shut the shell and told Adella to put it back wherever she found it. Adella did not understand what was going on until her mom explained that the oyster belonged to the Mer King's daughter, and it was given to her on her sixteenth birthday. That oyster had been passed down from many generations, and it was a big deal for the Mer King's family. After absorbing all of this information, Adella became very despondent because she had finally found an amazing treasure, but she could not keep it.

The next day, Adella woke up and saw that the pearl was glowing a fiery, red color. She did not know why the pearl was doing that, and she began to panic. Her heart was beating like a drum in a marching band. Despite her fear of the pearl, Adella slowly crept towards it and picked it up. As soon as she picked it up, the glowing came to a halt. Adella could not figure out what triggered the pearl to do that. She tried tapping it, shaking it, and even talking to it but nothing seemed to work. After a while, she put the shell back in her bag and got ready to return the shell back to the Mer King.

After taking two hours of precise makeup application, singing in the mirror, and choosing the perfect outfit, Adella was finally ready to head over to the Mer King's house to return the oyster. As she headed out, a sudden rush of anxiety hit her. Her hands became shaky, her breath was unsteady, and she felt paralyzed. She tried so hard to continue swimming, but she was stuck in the same spot for about five minutes, until she was able to reassure herself that everything was going to be okay. Adella felt a sudden burst of anxiety because she did not want the king thinking she stole the pearl and was a thief. She was able to calm herself down by talking to herself and saying that the king would be very understanding and appreciative for her being honest and returning the pearl to him.

Everyone in the town of Waverly, where Adella lives, knew that is was not an easy task to reach the Mer King's house. They warned her about the dangerous crooks and slithering sea monsters she would encounter along the way. Hearing all of this information started to discourage her from returning the pearl, but she kept swimming along hoping nothing bad would happen. Just as luck would have it, she was halted by a hair-raising, hideous sea monster. The sea monster was not like any regular sea monster. He had long, jagged teeth that could puncture skin like butter and small, beady eyes that felt like he was piercing through your soul. Adella immediately stopped in her tracks and listened to everything the monster told her to do. She was demanded to give him all of her money and anything else she had that was valuable. Just as she was about to give him the pearl, the sea monster heard the Waverly police blowing their loud, high-pitched siren indicating they were nearby, which caused him to scurry away, leaving the pearl safe with Adella. That event made Adella even more discouraged to return the pearl because it was becoming too much of a hassle and was dangerous.

Instead of giving up, Adella pushed through her fears and continued on her quest to return the pearl. Once she finally reached the Mer King's house, guards approached her and asked her what her reason was for wanting to see the king. As soon as she told them, they immediately led her to the Mer King's office. As the guards knocked on his door, Adella's heart dropped to her stomach, and she started to panic again. Before she could give into her fear, the door swung open and out came the Mer King, looking as handsome as ever with his long, curly hair and prominent muscles. The guards explained why Adella was there, and he instantly demanded to see the pearl. Once Adella handed him the pearl, tears began to swell up in his eyes, and he called for his daughter. When his daughter finally reached his office, he handed her the pearl, and she began to cry tears of joy.

Seeing these reactions from the Mer King and his daughter touch Adella's heart and she realized all of the fear and stress the journey caused her was worth it. She no longer wanted to be selfish and keep the pearl for herself. Adella never knew how capable she was of making someone to happy, and it inspired her to do it more often. After that day, she looked into volunteer work and spent more time pleasing other people and making them happy by just doing little things for them that made them feel cared for.

About the Author

Alicia Diaz is an eighteen-year-old college student who currently attends Fullerton College. She grew up in Anaheim, California with her two older brothers and was raised by her beautiful mother Loretta Diaz. She always hoped she would have a lot of people read her stories and now that dream is coming true. Alicia has always had a passion for writing, and she is very excited to have the honor of being published for the first time ever. Alicia's favorite style of writing is short stories that are very detailed and imaginative. She hopes that anyone who reads her short story *The Pearl* thoroughly enjoys it and recommends it to their friends and family. There is nothing better than having your hard work be appreciated by other people.

The Letter

Danilo Escobar

"The fear of death follows from the fear of life. A man who lives fully is prepared to die at any time."

Mark Twain

July 28, 2003

To whom it is of interest:

It was during the warm days of mid-July, when the days seemed to be longer and longer, so long that it felt as if it were an eternity for such to end and a new day to start. The sun would come out early at five in the morning, and it would not go down until seven in the evening. The days were long enough where you were able to wake up as late as you would like to and still have enough time left to do your chores, laundry, clean around the house and even run errands. Time seemed to be richly provided that the term "night time" never came to the minds of anyone during those days. Kids would have more than enough time to play outside their homes with their neighborhood friends.

Those were the days where you could wake up and feel the happiness flowing through the pleasant air throughout the entire neighborhood. Life was easy going and smooth since everyone was on some kind of vacation during those times, especially the little ones. When nighttime came along, in the urban areas, everyone would stay home, relax, and watch their favorite shows, while having dinner with their families. In the villages or towns, individuals would decide to sit outside and wait until the stars came out and let their beauty to be appreciated as they decorated the darkness of the magnificence of our sky. The young ones were the ones who took the most advantage of such long lengths of time because all they needed to focus on was enjoying their time away from school.

Life in the villages was and still is much simpler than in the city. It is simpler in every aspect. Traffic is not a problem at all. The only traffic the residents of such areas experience is while entering the urban areas; terrible drivers and rude individuals were nothing but a myth in these towns, where the rudest thing you could do and be part of was not to say hello or wave to the person walking by you or across the street from you.

Life in these town areas is as simple as it can get. You do not have to worry about watching over your kids because of the fear of someone passing by and taking from you to sell to a guy on a different continent for unimaginable purposes. But what if I told you the ones who you would have to look after were not even alive? While living in the villages, every parent in those areas knew about the terrible and sometimes even unbelievable myths that the woods would hide. The secrets that lay inside the trees and small forests were the secrets you in the city would have never believed until the day you and your children decided to move into the amazing town neighborhoods were everything seemed to be perfect. But, even perfect has faults at some point.

It all started when we moved for the summer from the urban city, which was located about 90 kilometers away from a small town where life seemed to be very calm and easy going. Individuals appeared to have a nice smile on their faces all the time. Houses were colorful and appealing, with flowers in the front yards, nicely decorated windows with beautiful colonial architecture, not only around the windows, but also around the door frames. Almost every house had a mailbox decorated with finger paint drawings in it, which showed the unique scent of every house in which young kids resided. A sensation of calmness and pure relaxation was flowing in the air, as soon as you stepped into the town. I wished it was our own place, so we could live there forever. Unfortunately, we could only reside there for a couple of weeks, while we visited our grandma for our summer break from school.

It was me, my brother Gerardo and, coincidently, my cousin with the same name as my brother. Every time we visited during the summer, we loved entering the woods and decided to go hiking and explore the new mysteries the woods and trees hid from us. Every time we decided to walk through the beautiful green forests, we always decided to take a different path without really minding if we got lost or not. In reality, one of our main purposes was to walk as far as possible to get lost, so we could be able to struggle and explore our way back. That was probably not the best idea we as teenagers could have had, but we never seemed to realize how much of a dangerous idea it was until the last summer we visited our grandmother before she passed away seven years ago…

It was like any other day at my grandmother's house. We would wake up to the scent of her delicious cooking. She would stuff us with as much food as possible, to the point where we were not able to walk for the next ten or twenty minutes. My brother and I loved sitting at the table. Sometimes, we competed to see how many pancakes we were able to eat. Right after stuffing ourselves with pancakes, beans, eggs, bacon, bread and plenty of cups of hot chocolate, my brother and I would get ready and walk towards our cousin's house who lived a couple houses down on the right from our grandmother's.

His house was just like our grandma's, with a beautiful antique Spanish colonial architecture decorating the interiors and exteriors of the house. His home was a pastel pink color, which combined perfectly with the white and pink roses planted in his backyard. As soon as we were close to Gerardo's house, we would not knock on the door. Instead, we would yell his name, and seconds later, he would come out ready to go on an adventure. He was our guide. He was barely nine years old, the youngest of us three. I was eleven, and my brother was fourteen. Even though he was the youngest, he was the sharpest when it came to finding the way back when we were lost. He knew the woods as if they were the palm of his hand. Sometimes though, his hand would get him lost in the woods at some points when we were exploring those places. After we met up with Gerardo, we decided to start our new adventure and see what new amazing places and views we could find.

It was ten in the morning when the sun was still getting ready to shine and warm our day. As soon as we entered the woods, a tropical scent surrounded us with humongous trees covering the top of our heads to the point where we could not see the light of the sun much anymore. Birds from far away could be heard. Little worms of different colors and ants were on the ground, along with other insects co-existing into their environment, which we had just invaded once again. We hiked several hills where they led to nowhere else than just a deadly drop where its end seemed to never be reached. Sometimes, we decided to kind of hang out around those hills and just throw rocks and wait until we could hear them fall at the bottom of it. But on many occasions, the rocks seemed to never hit the end of the drop.

While hanging around the drops, we sometimes also found trees, which had fallen off and disconnected from Mother Earth by ripping its roots apart. Those trees were so big that we were able to even go inside them while they were decaying and allowing Mother Nature to make holes in their trunks. One thing we liked about those places was that even though back in the villages everything seemed to be calm and quiet, in those places inside the woods, there was a different kind of quiet. It was so calm and relaxing that you could hear your own thoughts and sometimes even my brother's or cousin's thoughts while they were not even talking. There were no dangers to worry about, no school or homework to stress about, and it seemed to be our little secret place where we could go and relax.

But it was too good to be true. Along the amazing trees, flowers, plants, little animals, and amazing shade covering us from the sun, there was another side, which did not seem to add up. As we walked through these woods, something did not feel right. It always felt as if we had somebody walking right behind us, somebody or something which always watched us. At certain moments, it felt as if the trees were looking down on us with their huge trenches watching every step we made and every direction we took until a certain point. Maybe they were waiting for us to get lost as we usually did. But every time we did, it felt as if the woods did not want us to find our way back, as if the trees wanted us to stay in order for us to meet this something or someone who seemed to always follow us.

Our grandma would tell us stories as we grew up of how we were never supposed to enter these woods. Many of the villagers residing there, especially the ones who lived there for quite a long time like our grandma, knew about never stepping foot into those forests, but we still did anyway. Our adventurous personalities and seeking for curiosity forced us to break the rules and walk right in regardless of the dangers that we were exposing ourselves to.

Deep inside, I think we three always knew something was not right about that place. It was too calm and perfect to not have any defects. But we decided to ignore the doubting sensations because of our curiosity, also because deep inside we did not want to be the one who walked away because we were scared because then the teasing between each other would have started.

The last time we decided to go into the woods, things seemed to be as perfect as they could get. The weather was just right for us to not feel dehydrated during our little adventure. The trees did not seem to look down on us like other times, and there was no sensation of spookiness. I remember we arrived to a dead end at the top of a mountain where there was a house not so far away from us. It was about five minutes away in walking distance. Gerardo, my brother, suggested going to check it out, and I sure agreed to what he said, as I was the younger brother and I wanted to follow his footsteps on anything he would do.

We were about to go check the house out and maybe see if we could go inside it because it appeared to be abandoned. However, Gerardo, my cousin, suggested not to with a really serious voice. He even suggested we go back home as soon as possible because it was going to get late. It was midafternoon at around 12, right when the sun was barely starting to shine over our heads and starting to warm up the day for our adventure. His voice sounded scared and unpleasant, even though he was normally the calmest and bravest of all three when it came to exploring new places. That time he was concerned and urgent to get out of the woods. I asked him why he did not want to go in to inspect the abandoned house, and he furiously and anxiously replied to me, "Because we must go! We should not be here anymore!"

I could feel there was something wrong in his tone of voice. I had never heard him yell at me that way before. Then, Gerardo jumped into the conversation and tried to convince my cousin to come with us and look around the house. As the oldest one of all, he knew a better way to get around people and make them accept something they did not. He somehow convinced him by calmly telling him, "C'mon, big man. Let's go. We're just going to look around it. There is nobody here. What could go wrong?"

My cousin then agreed and calmed down a little bit, although he still felt as if something was wrong about that house in front of us. We were sitting on a huge trunk which had been cut off from a tree. It was probably as thick as my own height. The trunk felt as if it wanted to tell us a story, although that time the trees did not seem to pull us back away from our way out. That time, the trunk we were sitting on felt so comfortable and relaxing that it kind of felt as if it was trying to make us feel comfortable enough to not get up and decide to follow up with our inspection of checking out the spooky house.

Its windows were closed securely with racks of wood; the door was chained with a really thick chain and a lock that seemed to be a hundred years old. My brother Gerardo suggested going inside the house no matter its spooky structure and unattractive looks. I reached the door and the windows with the purpose of trying to find an entrance, but there was no success at all. My cousin Gerardo stayed off the porch area and kind of froze as soon as my brother kept trying to locate an entrance.

Then, my brother asked my cousin, "Hey, what is going on with you? Why are you being such a chicken today?"

My cousin nervously cried and asked, "You guys don't see it?"

"See what?" I exclaimed. I walked up to my cousin and asked him with an apprehensive tone in my voice, "What is it Gerardo? What is it we are supposed to see?"

He then lifted his right index finger and pointed at the top of the house at one specific window, which seemed to lead into the attic. We both happened to see what appeared to be a man who had hung himself. His clothes appeared to be from a past century. His face seemed to be in pain, and the body kept on swinging back and forth from the roof of the house. As my brother kept on trying to look for an entrance, I looked for the little sense of being alive at that moment inside me and yelled at him to stop and get away from the house as soon as possible.

In an upset tone of voice, he yelled, "What is wrong with the two of you today?" and then proceeded to walk towards me. As he got closer to me, just as my cousin, I lifted my right index finger and pointed at the same window, which showed the man hung from the roof of the attic in that old abandoned house.

Seconds after seeing the horrendous imagine through the window we should have never even looked at, the three of us were in such shock that once the man from the attic disappeared, our eyes could not believe what we had just seen, what had just happened, and we did not know what was about to happen after. We could not believe how we saw a man hanging in the attic with clothes which were not even from our time, and seconds later, the same man had disappeared from the window.

The three of us decided to run away and go back home, so we ran. It was around one in the afternoon by then; the sun was on our heads, making us feel deprived and dehydrated. The same route we took when we went into the woods seemed to never end that time. The trees surroundings us did not want us to leave that place once again, unlike the other times when we felt their frustration every time we left the woods. That time it was different. It was as if we had awakened something we weren't supposed to. The trees had woken up completely. The forest, which everyone in the town used to talk about and always warn others to never approach, had woken up, and most importantly, the demon, which controlled the elements which made up those forests, had finally seen a new prey for itself, a prey which that time was going to be us.

Soon after we decided to escape the woods for once and for all, the demon, the man, who we had previously seen at the house hung from·the attic, appeared to us right in front of us hanging from his neck, which was tied up from one of the trees. The tree seemed to not let us escape from the horrible and unspeakable nightmare we had just started encountering. Everywhere we went, the man would appear in front of us until we got to another dead end where the only way out seemed to be a 50 to 60 foot drop onto nothing but rocks at the bottom.

This is where the man seemed to want us to run to; he did not want us to escape anymore. It was waiting patiently for us to finally find out the home where he had hung himself decades ago, patiently waiting and captivating our attention and will for curiosity with the mysterious appearance the woods, trees and plants possessed.

Every summer we had gone to visit, explore, get lost and find our way back home, the demon had been patiently waiting for us until that day when it led us to his favorite place where he took away the souls of many young kids like me, my brother and cousin. It was playing with us. It ordered the trees to follow our footsteps each summer we decided to jump into a new adventure. It manipulated the woods in a manner where our attention was attracted to the secrets we wanted to discover, but we were never intended to know. The secret of why the place was so perfect, so quietly beautiful and relaxing was because no man alive dared to enter a footstep in those woods. No other human beings in their right senses made the choice to walk through the huge trees, which hid the secret of the demon residing in that area.

With no other way out than to either let ourselves be caught by the man or jump into the rocks waiting down the mountain, the man, the demon, revealed its eyes. He opened his eyes, and he did not seem to be dead anymore. His eyes reflected hell itself. It was an image that you cannot stop thinking about, not because of the content of it, but because of the huge trauma it caused you. Once you stared into his eyes, you felt the need to commit suicide due to the terrible things you experienced by staring into the dead soul of the demon.

I stared straight into his eyes. I saw and felt the pain he had suffered. I saw the true motives of his death and incentives of why he was so obsessed with our lives. It was a pain I could not explain nor had felt before. I felt the temptation to look away, but his pain and sadness made me addicted to keep on staring at his horrendous and hideous dead pupils.

Seconds after feeling his suffering, my body and spirit could not take such punishment anymore; that was when I decided to jump off that cliff. I remember looking at his eyes and telling myself I couldn't take it anymore. Then, I proceeded to look at my brother one last time in this human life and then followed by looking at my cousin as well. They both seemed terrified. Their faces expressed the fear I once felt once I saw the man hanging from the attic through that window. My cousin had warned us to go back home when he had the chance to; our grandma and many others back in the village told us not to ever go into the woods, but we never listened. We let our egos of knowing it all and our curiosity in seeking new mysteries to be discovered to make us go inside the forbidden place anyway.

I looked at them both once again and told myself that was the last time I was going to step foot into that place again, but then again my soul was already trapped there for eternity. With that last thought of the woods being my new home, I proceeded and jumped to my death, trying to escape the pain I saw in his eyes, the pain that now hunts me down every day and night. I can still feel the pain I experienced once my fragile body jumped onto those rocks. I can still taste the blood in my mouth and the pain from my broken ribs. Lastly, I can still hear their voices: my brother's and cousin's voice screaming of horror once they saw my body lying on those rocks covered in blood. I can still hear their last screams of help once the demon stole their souls away. He killed them both with no thought of compassion whatsoever. Personally, I do not know what was worse, to die under his power or to end your own life in such a painful way as I did.

The legend says that long time ago, on a sunny day during mid-summer, there was a child who would always hung out in these woods by himself. He was in between the ages of 9 and 12 and loved walking and hiking through the amazing trees, which provided him with shade. His mother had passed away from unknown causes shortly before he started spending time on his own in the woods. Legend says while spending time alone there, he could talk to his mother, and one day while making conversation with her, the young person decided to jump off a cliff, ending his life right on the spot. He committed suicide with the purpose of seeing his mother once again in person. His father, who found out about his son's death soon later that same day, was so devastated that he made a promise of never spending time away from his son again, so he decided to build his home in the same woods where his son used to play.

Weeks later, after already settling into his new home, the father could not live alone anymore; he could not take such pain anymore, so he decided to make a pact with the devil, which consisted of him killing himself in order for him to have the ability to maybe get his son back once again. On a lonely rainy night, when the pact was made at the house in the woods, the father made sure nobody would come into his home by locking it from the outside and inside and then walked up to the attic where he hung himself. By turning his soul to the devil, he then had the power to control the woods. The trees, rocks, and plants were all under his mercy and all allowed him to attract young children to play. The father liked to collect souls of those kids who reminded him of his dead son. He would hunt them down to the same spot where his son committed suicide. And those who were able to escape from getting their souls away could only escape by committing suicide before their soul was stolen from their bodies.

I have not seen my brother or my cousin since that last day we decided to adventure ourselves into the woods on that summer of 2003. I now wander in the woods on a daily basis hearing the screams of help of many who dare to go inside the forbidden place. I warn you: Do not come in here! Once you explore our mysteries, you cannot get enough until your soul belongs to him. Stay away! Follow my words, and do not let your children get near this place. Please, tell my grandma I am okay. Please, tell her I am sorry for not listening. If you are reading this letter, please tell her I am truly sorry for disobeying her word and leaving my brother and cousin alone at their moment of facing their death.

About the Author

Danilo Escobar is a well-determined writer, known by his peers for his high devotion to his goals. Regardless of his obstacles, such as transiting culturally from one country to another, he still managed to break language barriers and achieve his goals. He stands out for excellence in work ethic and professionalism. Danilo has earned several academic achievement certificates during his years in high school, and at just the age of twenty years old, as a college student, he is the author of *Hard Times in Life and Their Joys*, "The Little Boy who got His Childhood Destroyed," and "The Letter."

Following a Dream

Don Franco, Jr.

"All our dreams can come true,
if we have the courage to pursue them."

Walt Disney

Throughout my years in high school, my goal in life was to obtain a career in the field of medicine. The medical field has always sparked a level of interest to me since growing up as a child. With my continuous visits to the doctor's office as a child, I was able to observe how compassionate the doctors and nurses were to me. To this day, it astonishes me how nurses have the ability to help sick people. All people in the medical field would say that there is no greater joy than to help a sick patient, and if I were in their place nothing would make me happier than helping sick people.

All nurses have at least one thing in common: They want to help people. Not only do they play the role of caretaker for their patients, but in some circumstances, they can also be a friend, a confident, and a trusted adviser. It takes a special kind of person to fill all of those roles the way nurses and doctors do. I think my main source of inspiration to become a nurse comes from an innate desire to help people and care for them in times of need. I am also a person who thrives on being challenged, and I always have new goals to achieve. Nursing suits me, as few other careers offer as much diversity and learning opportunities.

As a freshman at La Quinta High School, there are three career based programs that the school offers. One of them happens to be an academy in the medical field. This was the perfect chance for me to explore the medical field. This academy was designed for anyone wishing to pursue a medical career and college. It combines technical skills, real world application of skills, and rigorous academics. The medical health academy accumulated hours that may be used for future programs that require experience or an internship. It can be documented in resumes, applications or programs, to gain an advantage over students that have no clinical or practical experience in the workplace. Therefore, it was great opportunity for me to acquire the benefits of this program.

The benefits that this program had to offer to the students of La Quinta High School were tremendous. The Medical Health Academy is not just a program that teaches you about the background information on becoming a nurse and doctor, but I've been told this program gives you a variety of opportunities that the medical field has to offer. The committed and hardworking student that I am, who is also very kind, shy and most importantly respectful to my teachers and fellow students, I would have been the most dedicated student to this program. I really wanted the benefits that the Medical Health Academy of La Quinta High School has to offer. I know am the right student for this Academy.

The minute I got my hands on the application, the following day, I returned the application. The following week, they began conducting interviews, which lasted for several weeks. I went through the interview with positive energy and confidence. I went early before the appointed time and the interview was conducted as a group, with no less than ten students. The Medial Health Academy had its own building on the campus of La Quinta High School. The atmosphere inside the building was completely different. It looked exactly like a hospital would be pictured, with more than fifteen hospital beds surrounded by curtain lined up against the walls.

The lady, who conducted the interviews, took us to her office. She then introduced herself as Ms. Pedersen. She continued giving us background information about the academy, the rules that were expected to be followed, and how she could only have a certain number of students to join the program. As the interview was being conducted, everyone got a chance to introduce themselves to Ms. Pedersen. Afterwards, she asked each of us a special question, "Why do you want join the program?" When it was my turn to answer the question, I had a sense of confidence. I started to talk about how I wanted to get more in depth in cancer, especially breast cancer, ever since my mom was diagnosed with breast cancer and knowing the fact that my proud mother was one of the lucky ones to be a breast cancer survivor.

One day, I'm determined to help other people and save the lives of other men and women from this deadly cancer. I continued by saying I wanted to achieve my goal of becoming a nurse, X-ray technician, or even a veterinarian. I wanted to explore the medical field, be mentored by weekly medical speakers, and get "hands on" training. I want to be able to have a team of teachers who will work together and help me build my successful future. I also looked forward to job shadowing, as a junior, then internship, as a senior.

As weeks passed by and the interviews were all done, Ms. Pedersen finally posted the people who would enroll into the program the following year. I desperately went to check if my name was on that list. As I was approaching the list, my hands started to sweat. I started to get a gut feeling inside of me that I did not make it into the program. I started to scan through the list to check if my name was on there.

Suddenly, my heart stopped, and I began to walk away in despair. As time progressed, I came to a point in my life and realized that I do not need their program to get to what I desire to be in life. Despite the rejection and despite what the program had to offer me, I will always remember that success comes in many different options and methods, to get to where I want to be. It just gives me motivation to succeed even higher and most importantly to follow my dreams.

About the Author

Don Franco, Jr. was born on August 17, 1997 in Palm Springs, California. He successfully graduated from La Quinta High School, class of 2016. He is currently a student at College of the Desert Community College, located in Palm Desert, California. His plans are to acquire a degree in Health Science, then transfer to University of California, Los Angeles, to further his education. In addition, he will undergo a career in the medical field to become a registered nurse. He is passionate about the needs of other people. The main source of his inspiration to become a nurse comes from an innate desire to help people and care for them in times of need. He thrives on being challenged and always has new goals to achieve. Mr. Franco is a committed and hardworking student, who is also very kind, dedicated and, most importantly, respectful to his professors, fellow students, and the community.

Stacey's Knee

Kacey Fuentes

"Life, love, stress, and setbacks."

Atmosphere

Nothing hurt more my soul more than seeing my dear older sister Stacey flushed in agony due to a cheer stunt gone wrong during summer practice. At ten years old, my summer days were spent in my one-bedroom apartment with my family of five, or spent outside enclosed with the gates of our apartment complex. Every day was the same as the last. My morning ritual consisted of sleeping until I could no longer stand being in the same stuffy room, feeling every crevice of my body stick to each other as if they were glued together and then spending the day with my shy five-year-old sister Abigail, and strong willed, yet loving mother who took the summer off from work to be with my sisters and me. My mom would leave every day at two o'clock in the afternoon and again at five o'clock in the evening to drop and pick Stacey up from the tough, long, and physically challenging, high school cheer practice.

This particular day, started off as an average summer day in my home. The sun stood high, beaming into every window of the apartment. Nothing made more noise in our apartment than the roar of the wind blowing from the giant, old school industrial fan, not even the noise of cartoons playing all day long for my younger sister. At noon, our mom made us our favorite lunch, turkey sandwiches with baby carrots and a whole lot of ranch. As I ate, I remember sitting at the kitchen table, admiring how big the sunflowers in our backyard had grown. As always, at two in the afternoon my mother dropped Stacey off at cheer practice. When she returned, all was calm and quiet, until the clock struck four, when my mom's phone began to ring repeatedly from an unknown source. Bothered with the solicited phone calls, I finally picked up the phone. Without letting the unidentified caller get a word in, I asked him/her with as much attitude you could expect from ten-year-old girl to stop calling that number. Unfortunately, I did not manage to get the unidentified caller to stop. He continued to call. Finally, my stern mother decided that enough was enough. The next time her phone rang, she answered herself. It turned out that it had been Stacey's cheer advisor calling all along. There had been an accident. He informed my mom that she needed to head to the high school right away. I looked at my mother, and I could see the fear in her eyes. She quickly packed my younger sister and me into the back of the car, and we flew to the scene.

As we approached the high school, I could the see the mob of Fullerton fire trucks and ambulances. I walked out of the car in a daze. I could not my wrap my head around what was actually happening right in front of my eyes. I saw I was not the only one feeling that way. All of the other teenage cheerleaders were in disbelief. The cheer advisor I had spoken to on the phone earlier began to lead us to the back of the ambulance. As we inched closer, I could hear the suffering in my sister's cry. I only caught a glimpse of Stacey before she was taken away to the emergency room, but I could tell she was in a great deal of pain. Tears were pouring down her flushed cheeks, as she yearned for our mom's comfort. Her left leg was wrapped in a cardboard brace, and her shoes were torn apart completely by the emergency medical technicians, so they could assess the injury to her leg.

Because it was only my mom, younger sister, and I that came down to the high school, we had to meet my older sister and the ambulance at the hospital. When we arrived, that is when my injured sister's pain began to intensify. As she was admitted into the emergency room, Stacey's shriek of pain alarmed the nurses and the lingering patients. Two nurses rushed to her side and immediately inserted an intravenous while assuring her she would be okay. To put her pain at ease, the nurses wanted to administer morphine to Stacey but did not because my mother feared it would be too strong for her daughter's petite body to handle. So instead, they administered a large dose of Vicodin, which lead Stacey to feeling nauseous and vomit. In the panic of it all, our mother realized that it was too much for young children to witness. We were escorted out into the waiting room where we waited for our dad to come get us. An hour went by. I spent the time cradling my little sister, trying my best to explain to her what had happened. I barely understood myself. I had never experienced a family emergency that I was old enough to remember. I did not know how it would affect Stacey and our family as a whole. I knew she was hurt, but I did not know the severity of her injury. I had so many unanswered questions.

It was ten past eight when my dad, younger sister, and I arrived home. I was tired and filled with more emotions than I had ever even known existed. I waited patiently for Stacey to return home. I fell asleep while waiting, but was awakened by the noise my mom made struggling to bring Stacey into the house because she was on crutches and had a huge, heavy white brace to secure her leg from moving. Stacey was softly whimpering, she felt helpless because of her situation. I could tell by her expression that she had been physically, mentally, and emotionally drained. Her rosy cheeks had faded to a subtle fair tone. Her big dark brown eyes were now irritated and swollen with the many tears that were shed that evening.

Before going to bed, my mother explained to me that Stacey's knee had dislocated. She was the flyer in her cheer stunts. While practicing a stunt that day, something went wrong when she went up that caused too much pressure for her left leg to handle, so her knee cap snapped out of place. My mom showed me the x-rays to demonstrate what had happened. When she held them up to the light, I could see that Stacey's patella was on the far left side of her leg. Seeing my older sister injured broke my heart. I did not understand why such a bad accident had to happen to her. A part of me felt useless. There was nothing that I could say or do to make her predicament better.

About the Author

Kacey Fuentes is eighteen years old and grew up in Fullerton, California with her family of five. Fuentes is currently attending Fullerton College as a full-time student. She has high hopes to find and pursue a career that she is truly passionate about. Outside of school, Kacey's hobbies include going to as many concerts as she can, going to Disneyland with her two sisters, and anything that she can do with her family. Kacey Fuentes has never looked into writing as a career path, but she is overjoyed to be participating in this book. Participating in the book has given her a new level confidence, as well as the determination to give all tasks of life her best effort.

The Savior of the World

Eli Giancanteri

"I have said these things to you, that in me you may have peace.
In the world you will have tribulation.
But take heart; I have overcome the world."

John 16:33 (Jesus)

The story I am about to tell you is a story well known around the world, yet it is a story that is not taken to heart and believed by a lot of people in our day and age. It is the story of Jesus Christ. The Holy Bible is the book this story comes from. It was written by many different people, including Jesus' apostles and various prophets who God appointed. The story begins in a tiny, dirty manger in Bethlehem where Jesus was born.

When Jesus was born, he fulfilled an old testament prophesy. He was foretold to be born in a manger in Bethlehem, born of a virgin, and his name will be called Immanuel. This virgin the Bible speaks of is Mary. She was visited by the angel Gabriel who told her that she would give birth to a son, to name him Jesus, and that he will rule as king for all eternity and save humanity. She was perplexed at first since she was only a teenager at the time and never had any sexual relations with her husband Joseph. However, Gabriel told her that the Lord will come upon her and make this possible. So, she submitted to God's will after hearing this.

People would expect the Son of God to come down on a white, majestic horse, holding a massive sword with beams of light and rolls of thunder coming out of the sky. He is the king of the world after all. So, why did he come in the manner which he did? He came as a humble servant, as a man, born in a manger full of animals and filth. This shows he was not concerned with a glorious entrance or demanding praise from every human being of the world because of his glory. He had a much bigger plan ahead of him that God had given him: to take on every sin of man and put it on the cross with him.

The people of Bethlehem knew he was the Messiah of prophesy. Three kings from a distant land even came to bring him gifts. They were astronomers who followed the star of Bethlehem to see the birth of the king.

After his birth, Jesus grew up like any Jewish boy would. He grew up in Jerusalem. The Bible is not too detailed about his childhood other than explaining how when he was twelve, he was having deep theological and spiritual conversations with the teachers of the law in the temple. This shows even at a young age, he was divinely and spiritually gifted by his father, who is God. Then after this, the Bible goes straight into Jesus' adulthood. The first thing it records him doing is getting baptized by John the Baptist. He was baptized in the Jordan River. Although John was baptizing Jewish people for confession of sins and a chance to get right with God, we know Jesus doesn't need repentance of sins. He is God. So why did he get baptized? In his own words he said, "Let it now be so, for thus it is fitting for us to fulfill all righteousness." Even though he had no sins to repent of, it shows that the righteousness he wanted to fulfill was the righteousness not required of him, but of every sinful man.

After his baptism in the Jordan, he traveled all throughout Judea, Samaria, and Galilee, fulfilling his Father's will of seeking and saving the lost. He performed many miracles and taught numerous sermons and parables to people and gained many followers. However, he also developed many enemies, especially the Pharisees. These were the Jewish scholars and teachers in that time. They hated him because he threatened their security, prestige, and wealth in the Roman society. Anyone who took heed to Rome's political and military authority, they could go about their business and do whatever. The Pharisees wanted to keep it that way. Jesus rebuked them many times, calling them hypocrites because they taught things, yet didn't do it themselves. He also rebuked them for being too concerned about their ranking, money, and respect of the people when it is really about helping people to see the real leader and Rabbi, who is Jesus Christ.

Jesus had appointed twelve apostles or in other words, followers of him, and gave them the great commission which was to preach the gospel across the nations. This commission carries over for Christians to obey as well. Most of the apostles wrote their own books of the Bible and did many miracles and led people to Christ as well. One of the apostles Judas, betrayed Jesus for thirty pieces of silver and turned him in to the Pharisees, while Jesus was praying in the Garden of Gethsemane. The Pharisees turned him over to Pilate, who was the governor of Rome at that time and accused him of blasphemy and false accusations that he is the Messiah sent by God or "The King of the Jews." The crowd shouted to crucify him at the trial. Pilate had no choice but to follow the people's wish, even though he found no evidence to crucify him.

The very people that welcomed Jesus with much celebration and joy into Jerusalem are the same people that sent him to the cross. They turned away from their Messiah. However, Jesus knew this fate was coming. It was his whole purpose for coming into this world. He told his disciples that he would be crucified but would rise again on the third day and why that was going to take place. He knew it was the Father's will, to die for the sins of mankind. Jesus was so scared to do this he was sweating blood and asked God to allow the responsibility to pass from him. He didn't want to experience the pain and suffering. But, he knew he had too.

He wore a crown of thorns on his head, nails were pierced through his hands and feet, he was whipped, mocked and beaten, then hung on a cross to die. Jesus was innocent, and Pilate and the Pharisees knew that. Pilate was just following the will of the people, while the Pharisees wanted to keep their fame and prestige in Rome. Jesus died to forgive every single sinner of the world. The very death that we deserve, he paid the price instead, so that we can be free from our sins and live forever with Him in eternity. He even forgave the very people that put him on the cross! He said, "Father, forgive them. For they know not what they do." When Jesus died, Joseph, of Arimathea, buried him in a tomb and sealed it. But low and behold,

Jesus rose again on the third day just as he foretold! He then ascended to heaven after forty days of revealing himself to everyone. Now, he sits at the right hand of the Father. This truly is the Messiah!

About the Author

Eli Giancanteri is eighteen years old and lives in Grand Terrace, California. He has a big heart for people and the Lord. He grew up in a Christian home and learned the ways of being a true Christian. As he got older, he better understood who and what Jesus is and how big of an impact He has in Eli's life. Having compassion and love for people has always been one of Eli's most important morals, and he hopes his story will spark an interest or desire to know more about God and His love for you. Eli is also a determined, goal-driven, and motivated person who strives to do his best in everything he does. He is looking forward to one day being able to express his love for people and helping others by being a firefighter.

Growing Up Too Fast

Destiny Green

"You never know how strong you are until being strong is the only option you have."

Bob Marley

"Ahhhhh." she screams as she gave birth to a baby girl. She had brown skin and bold baby blue eyes. Her name was Vanessa. Everyone in the hospital thought Vanessa was the best baby they ever laid hands on. She did not cry too much, only when she was hungry. Vanessa's mother was able to leave the hospital the very next day. June 2, 1996, Vanessa was checked out the hospital. "Off she goes home," says the nurse with the long black hair. Hearing, "Surprise," as they walked into their home. Her whole family was there waiting to meet the new baby girl. Vanessa's eyes opened wide as she looked at faces she had never seen. Months went by, and Vanessa went from a baby who did not cry to a baby who always cried. Vanessa's mother worked three jobs with very long hours, just to feed her baby girl. The late night cries and early morning stress was too much to handle. So, she decided to give Vanessa up for adoption because she could not handle the pressure of motherhood anymore. December 8, 1997, Vanessa finally got to meet her foster parents. They gave her a life her birth mother was not able to give her.

Years went by, and it was Vanessa's fifteenth birthday. She invited all of her close friends and family to celebrate her special day. Outside someone was screamed, "No, I need to see my daughter." Vanessa was confused and did not know who the crazy lady outside her house is looking for. Vanessa walked outside her house and said to the lady, "Who are you and why are you here?" The crazy lady responded, "I am your mother, and I'm here because I miss my baby girl." Vanessa gave a confused and lost look to her foster parents. The foster parents did not say a word but removed the crazy lady from outside their home. Vanessa did not believe what the crazy lady had said and enjoyed the rest of her day. The very next day, her foster parents wanted to have a talk with her. They sat down at the kitchen and began to explain what happened at Vanessa's birthday party. Vanessa stared out the kitchen window as her foster parents said, "We are not your biological parents." Tears began to roll off her chubby cheeks. She was hurt and upset because she felt as if her whole life was a lie and that she had grown up with a family that wasn't hers.

Vanessa took it upon herself to find the lady from the party again. Vanessa went to grocery stores, train stations, and hospitals trying to find her. One day, Vanessa was walking down the street, and she saw the crazy lady from the party again. But, that time she didn't look too well. Vanessa and the crazy lady sat down on a bench and talked about her past life. Vanessa began to cry as she spoke. The lady began to tell Vanessa that she was her biological mother. She froze as if her world had come to an end. She wanted answers.

After she talked with her biological mother, she went home to get answer from her foster parents. "We never wanted to hurt you. We just didn't know when the time was right to tell you about your mother," said her foster parents as Vanessa packed her clothes. "Where are you going?" asked Vanessa's parents. "I'm going to stay with my mother," said Vanessa. Her foster parents were not too happy about her decision, but they gave her a chance to make her own decision. She moved in with her biological mother, really not knowing who she was. So after she moved in, she then realized her mother used drugs.

Vanessa was only sixteen years old when she dropped out of high school and decided to take care of her biological mother. Her biological mother was diagnosed with cancer. A couple of years went by and her mother passed away. She finally got to feel part of herself. Vanessa wanted to get away from everything and everyone. So, she decided to leave the small town called Brawley. She's in the Big Apple now, New York City. She did not know anyone in the city. She was alone with no money and nowhere to go. Vanessa became homeless. One day, she was laying on the dirty ground when an older man approached her. He introduced himself as Jeff. He asked her why was she out in the streets alone. From that day, they became good friends. He helped her get an apartment on the 26th floor and a black jeep with a sun roof. She had everything she ever wanted. She soon fell in love with him.

Love turned into hate within months. He started beating her. She did not try to leave him because he would always apologize, but the apologies became frequent. He would beat her so bad that her face would begin to bleed. She had no one to turn to or anyone to talk to. She was alone. Days went by and all she could think about was if she never left her foster parents or what if she had never met her biological mother.

On August 24, 2013, Jeff got laid off at his job, and he came home furious. Vanessa was in the kitchen making dinner when he came home. He approached her and pushed her against the wall and began to say, "They fired me." Vanessa did not know what to do because she did not have a job or any money. He then proceeded to check his saving account and saw it only had $15.68. Jeff started to throw knifes, glass, and anything that was in arm's reach. "I'm sorry," said Vanessa, in a hysterical voice. He did not want an apology from her, so he beat her until she blacked out.

Hours later, she woke up on the kitchen floor in a pile of blood. She went into the restroom and cleaned herself up. After, she walked up the stairs to the bedroom looking for Jeff. She found him lying on the ground with pills scattered on the floor. She started pacing and called 911. When the ambulance arrived, they pronounced Jeff dead. Her heart was broken, but she was relieved because he could not hurt her anymore.

Days went by, and Vanessa got a job at Lowe's. She had been throwing up and feeling sick, but she did not know why. So, she went to the doctor and learned she was pregnant. She was happy and filled with joy to be having a baby. On September 1, 2016, Vanessa has now worked at Lowe's for three years and has a beautiful young son.

About the Author

Destiny Monae Green was born on December 22, 1997. She was born and raised in a small town called Brawley, CA. She is a young, gifted African American woman with many hopes dreams. She is currently attending College of the Desert, to achieve her Associates Degree in Early Childhood Education. After she receives her AA in Early Childhood Education, she plans to move out of state to continue school at a university.

Real Life Hero

Erika Gudino

Until you have lost a very dear pet
It's hard to feel the grief one begets.
But I know the sadness you are going trough
For I have worn those very same shoes.
You look around and see a big hole;
Your home empty, your heart not whole.
But day by day may the fading tears
Bring smiling memories year after year.

John and Jenny were just beginning their life together. They were young and in love, with a perfect little house and not a care in the world. They decided to start a new life and moved to West Palm Beach, Florida to initiate the project of building their family. John was a little nervous because his wife Jenny was anxious to have a baby, and he was not sure about parenting.

One night, John surprised his wife with a lovely large orchid flower with purple and cream leaves. Jenny was so happy; she thanked John by throwing her arms around his neck and kissing him.

"Be careful not to overwater it," John warned.

After a couple days, John asked Jenny about the plant and she replied, "It died. I think I put a lot of water in it." Then, she got the real issue: "If I can't even keep a plant alive, how am I ever going to keep a baby alive?" She looked like she might start crying. John thought maybe a dog would be good practice and started looking in newspapers.

The next day, John brought home a wiggly yellow fur ball of a puppy. It was a gold Labrador retriever; Jenny could not believe she had a little baby. They decided to name the puppy "Polo." After several months, Polo quickly grew into a barreling, ninety-seven-pound brute of a Labrador retriever, a dog like no other. It was a little hard for John and Jenny that Polo was a hurricane. Polo was not obedient. If he were alone at home, he would destroy everything around. Also, there were many visits to the veterinarian and many pills to calm him down. The dog was becoming a problem. John thought it would be a good idea to enroll Polo in a school of obedience for dogs, but that was not a good idea because Polo failed every class. And yet, Polo's heart was pure. Just as he joyfully refused any limits on his behavior, his love and loyalty were boundless. Over time, John and Jenny learned to live with the antics of Polo and giving him unconditional love.

Polo was their first baby and one of the most important things in their life. When Jenny discovered she was pregnant and gave the news to John, they could not believe they would be parents. With the arrival of the baby, Polo was very excited and did not want to separate from him.

One day, John decided to barbecue at their backyard, while the baby and Polo were sleeping in the bedroom. Jenny was outside helping John get everything ready when they heard the baby crying. They both tried to run inside to get to their baby, but they couldn't open the door. They realized the house was on fire. John called 911 for help, and Jenny was desperately trying to get inside, but the smoke was too heavy, and the door started falling. Jenny was crying uncontrollably and had lost all hope of seeing her child again.

Finally, the firefighters arrived on the scene. The house had heavy fire burning from both the first and second floors. They could hear the baby crying and acted quickly. It was not easy to get to the second floor where Polo and the baby were. After a long time of struggle, the firefighters got into the house and started looking for the baby. When they finally got to the bedroom, they could not believe what they saw. The baby was kept relatively safe by Polo, as he used his body to shield the infant from the flames. In turn, he only suffered burns on his arm and side. Polo and the baby were taken to the hospital immediately as well as John and Jenny because they had suffered minor burns on their hands and face when trying to enter the house to save their baby.

After reviewing the baby, the doctor said he would recover, but he must be in the hospital for a couple of weeks. John and Jenny were so grateful to Polo that he had saved the life of her baby, but they were very worried about whether or not know if Polo would recover.

After a week, the baby was ready to come home. But Polo was still severe, as he had inhaled all the smoke and had been close to the flames that had burned his body and destroyed his lungs. The vet told

John that Polo was suffering a lot and would not be a normal dog anymore. He would require much care, and it would be very costly. John was devastated and did not know what to do. John could let Polo recovered slowly, but he would not be the same and would also have pain for the rest of his life, or he could let Polo go, so he could rest in peace. It was very difficult for John and Jenny to make the decision. Polo was part of their lives. They had loved him since he was a puppy, and they didn't want to lose him.

With all the pain in his heart, John decided to let Polo go. That day, John and Jenny were in the room with Polo. They could not hold back the tears and the pain they felt. With tears in his eyes, John said to Polo: "I hope you know how much I loved you all of your life. You were always there when I needed you. Through life or death, I will always love you." After his words, Polo moved his tail, and he closed his eyes. Polo was gone. John and Jenny were very sad, but at the same time, they knew their friend was resting in peace, and he would be always in their hearts forever. He showed them what love can do. Polo had given his life for the baby who meant everything to John and Jenny. Polo became a hero and a symbol of true love.

About the Author

Erika Gudino a twenty-one year old college student living in Palm Desert, California. She is native of Barstow, California and was raised in Mexicali, BC Mexico. While she lived in Mexicali, she graduated from high school. She went to a beauty school for six months and earned her certificate as a nail technician and started her first job in a beauty salon. Erika had a passion for animals and always wanted to learn new things. Also, she became a certified dog groomer. When she became an adult, she went back to California and started college. She is studying to be a registered nurse while raising her two-year-old child.

Reunited

Urooj Khan

*"Nothing is permanent in this wicked world,
not even our troubles."*

Charlie Chaplin

The dark-haired girl was fast walking away from the group that was touring the town, picking up their phones or wallets from their pockets as she went by. He noticed her from afar; he was not much of a person to go and confront, but just observe. Eric decided to go back home. He turned on the silver Mercedes Benz he was in and drove off. The girl, Jackie, was not so unaware of the silver Mercedes she had seen around. She hoped it was not an undercover cop. Jackie wanted to figure out why the car was following her, but at that moment, she wanted to see how much she made. She went into the narrow alley, counted the money from the wallets, and went to get lunch before it was dark. Not knowing when she could see the silver Mercedes again, she started planning what to say and how to react if it were an undercover police officer.

Eric knew she was smart, but he did not realize she knew he was following her around. He still did not know how to tell her what he knew about her. He looked in the full-size mirror at his reflection. While the sun was setting, he was thinking of how he could approach her. Jackie knew of a cozy place to sleep, but she had to get there before any other person could take her spot. She was glad she could rest on a full stomach. The city was getting dark; the shadows were all displayed on the tall buildings. She appreciated the view she had the pleasure of seeing, as she went on her way.

After getting to the place that she had slept in for many nights, she lay down on her back and thought about her life – how she got to where she was and what the future would hold. All she remembered was being in a hospital-like place for kids. She never got along with other kids and did not want to either. Then, she went with a friendly couple to their house for some time. After that, she was with a single mom in an apartment, but she always returned to that institution for kids. It was nice and colorful, but it did not feel nice to stay there. When she was old enough to leave, she had nowhere to go, so she made herself a bed out of objects she found in neighborhoods of wealthy people and started pickpocketing as a means to get food and water. Jackie questioned if life would be different for her or if that was all she would do.

One day, instead of going to college, Eric was at home in his lavish room doing his homework. The sun was shining brightly facing his room. While he was working on his laptop, it seemed to be really hot, so he went to open one of the large windows. He opened it and before turning back to continue his work, he saw Jackie. Eric did not know who she was, but she looked familiar. By the time he went down the spiral staircase and out of the enormous house, she was out of sight.

The next time he saw her was in the market place. He was passing by when he happened to look her way. She was sitting on a curb looking at the people around her. Eric watched as she got up, passed by a business man having his coffee, but after passing by him, she had a thick, leather men's wallet in her hands. He realized she had found what she was looking for. He understood that she might be in a bad situation and decided to go on as if he did not know or see anything. After thinking about the matter over numerous times, he wanted to meet with her and talk, but to that day, he still had not been able to do that. Weeks of following her around made him feel uneasy, but he had to know about her.

It was a warm, busy Saturday in the already crowded market. Jackie knew that was the perfect time to score. Eric felt Jackie knew that and went to the market. By the time Eric got there, Jackie had already gotten a watch from a snooty-looking man, while he was arguing with an elderly shopkeeper. Jackie saw the silver Mercedes show up. She hid to see if the person would come out, as she never got to see this person's face, as the windows were tinted. A familiar looking man with dark brown hair and round trendy sunglasses, that covered his eyes, got out of the car. He took them off and was looking around the market. Jackie thought he was dressed extremely dressy and too rich to be a policeman. She came out from her hiding place and walked confidently with long strides to the man to find out why he had been following her for the past month.

Eric decided he was tired of hiding and wanted to talk to her that day. As he got out of the car, she disappeared. He was puzzled as to where she went as he had just seen her. He did not have to be confused for long, as she appeared out of nowhere right in front of him. She saw that his eyes were dark brown exactly like hers, and they just stared at each other. When she was closer to him, she realized he did look familiar, really familiar, but she could not figure out how she knew him. She was baffled as to how she would know the person driving the expensive car, wearing designer sunglasses and clothes. Eric had never seen her up close, and he finally believed the files he had found.

"You're my sister," said Eric, as he handed her the file. Jackie was stunned as she took the manila folder and opened it. Eric and Jackie were both from the same orphanage and had come from the same home originally because they were siblings. Eric was adopted by a wealthy family, and Jackie was left to fend for herself. She realized why he looked familiar. He was all that she had when her parents passed away, but she was too young to remember any of it.

About the Author

Urooj Khan is sixteen years old. She is the youngest of five siblings. Her parents are from Mumbai, India. This is her first year at Fullerton College. She is majoring in Biology. She is planning to transfer to a four-year university here in California. She has always enjoyed reading, swimming, and spending time with her friends and family, and now, she is interested in writing as well.

How I Got a Cat

Alicia Loredo

"Good things can come from unexpected places."

Last Man

It was the last week of high school. My mom and her boyfriend were out of town on a trip to Mexico, which left my brother and me with the house all to ourselves. One day, I came home to find my bother in our backyard staring at the fence. I went outside, and I asked him what he was staring at, to which he replied with an abrupt "Shh!" I was confused at first, but once I got closer to the fence, I began to hear tiny meows. After identifying the sound, I began to look for the source of the tiny meows. That is when my brother pointed to a gap between the fence that separated our house from the alley and one that kept trees from growing on our lawn. Hidden in that spot, there were about five of the cutest kittens I had ever seen. Three of the kittens were all black, and the rest were white. All of them had bright baby blue eyes.

I looked to my brother and asked him, "What should we do?" He shrugged his shoulders and went inside the house. My brother and I knew better than to remove the kittens from the fence. If we did, then our scent would be all over those kittens, and the mother would not want to take care of them. I then followed my brother back into the house. A few hours passed by, and I decided to go outside and check on the fence kittens. All of them are gone except one small black cat. I looked all around the backyard, but none of the other kittens were to be found. It looked as if the little black cat that was left behind was the runt of the litter, and the mother had left it behind.

In nature, mothers will often do this to their young if they believe that they will not survive in the wild. I went inside and grabbed a shoe box and a rag. After, I went back outside to where the small kitten was. Using the rag, I attempted to grab the kitten and put it inside the shoe box. It was not an easy task at first because the kitten was so frightened at the sight of me.

Once I finally got the kitten in the box, I took it inside. Unsure of what to do next, I proceeded to google everything I needed to know about caring for a young kitten. My brother and I were prepared to care for that kitten until it was big enough to give away. We gathered all the necessary supplies needed for the little kitten after a quick stop at PetSmart.

I knew once my mom came home from her vacation, the kitten would have to leave. My mother, brother, and I had allergies when it came to cats. My mother's allergies were more severe than the rest of ours. For the next few days, my brother and I would take turns caring for the kitten. We kept the kitten in the shoe box, in the corner of our living room, on the couch. While I was finishing school, my bother would watch the cat, and once I got home, I would watch the cat. The kitten was too young to eat dry or wet food, so we had feed it with a bottle. There was a special formula that is used when feeding young cats, similar to baby formula. Taking care of the kitten was not a challenge. At that age the kitten wasn't very active. The majority of the time, the kitten would be eating and sleeping.

The week went by fast, and it was Friday. I was done with school until the graduation ceremony, and my mom was expected to come home that night. My mom came home around 10pm. We were happy to see she made it home safe. She began to talk about all the things she did on her trip to Mexico. It was not long before she noticed a mysterious shoe box in our living room. She approached the box and opened it. She was surprised to see a little black fuzzy kitten sleeping in the box. I explained what had happened to the kitten, and to my surprise, she understood and let us continue taking care of the kitten. She let me care for it until we found a good home for the little cat. Despite being allergic to cats, my mom enjoyed having the cat around the house. She enjoyed bottle feeding the cat most of all. With time, we figured out if I bathed the kitten often, we are all less likely to have allergies.

Tuesday was the day of my graduation ceremony. I graduated from Fullerton Union High School. It was a big and nice ceremony. A lot of friends and family showed up to it. After the ceremony, everyone came over to our house for dinner. It was a great dinner; everyone was enjoying themselves. Everyone also admired the kitten that was temporarily staying at our house. One of my cousins then asked me if I was going to keep the kitten. I found it an appropriate time to ask my mom if she would let me keep the cat instead of giving it away. Surprisingly, her reply was yes. She said I could keep the kitten only if I take care of it and bathe it regularly. Without hesitation, I agreed to my mom's conditions.

The following Saturday, we took the cat to the family vet to get all of its necessary shots and vaccinations. That is when we found out the gender of the cat was male. It was more difficult than I expected to determine the gender of cats while they are young. I decided to name him Julian, after the lead singer in my favorite band. After Julian's vaccinations, we bought him a blue collar with a name tag. We also got him cat toys and a cat tree. Lastly, we got him a litter box and a large black cat bed to officially welcome him into his new permanent home. My mom and my brother enjoy having Julian around. We are all glad to have him as part of our home.

About the Author

Alicia Loredo graduated from Fullerton Union High school, in July 2016. She has always been fond of animals since she was a little girl. She currently owns two cats, two dogs, and three birds. While Alicia is not taking care of her animals, she likes to spend her time painting or playing piano. In the future, she hopes to find happiness and serenity wherever life takes her.

The Footsteps

Alma Munguia

"Monsters are real, ghosts are real too.
They live inside us, and sometimes, they win."

Stephen King

I still remember the first time I heard the footsteps. I remember it like it was yesterday. It was a warm, October evening. The leaves were turning; homes were decorated with spider webs, ghouls and pumpkins. I was walking home through the entrails of the city. It had been a long hectic day at work. I left work that night hungry and exhausted. Normally, I would take the long way home, the scenic route. I sure did love that route. I would wander on the nice side of town, pass all of our historical landmarks, the creek and the fields. Tonight, I was too exhausted to take that route. I just wanted to be home. So, I took the short way.

I was cutting through one of the sketchy alleyways near my job when I first heard them. The alleys weren't a nice place for a young girl to go through at night. There were all sorts of low-life people in this area. The downtown area was known to hold its fair share of gang members and violent junkies. So, you can imagine how terrified I was when I heard the footsteps.

I was walking through an alley, nearly halfway to the end when I began to hear someone walking behind me. I was immediately filled with terror. I remember my mind construing the worst scenarios possible. I had no doubt in my mind that at any given moment something bad was going to occur. I began to pick up my pace. I was walking faster and faster. Yet the footsteps were picking up. They were following me. Whoever was following me was sure to get me.

My heart was beating out of my chest. My breathing had become rapid and shallow. I was horrified. I began to take off as rapidly as my body allowed me. I was ready to run a quick turn to the right at the end of the alleyway. When I was about to reach the corner, I turned my head back and looked at what was behind me. To my amazement, there was no one. Not a single soul was in that alleyway. I sprinted all the way home, thanking God for saving me and sending whoever my harasser was on a different route. It wasn't until weeks later that I discovered what was following me home that day wasn't human, and it wasn't the end.

The footsteps would appear at odd times throughout the day. At first it took me three weeks to hear the footsteps again after my first encounter. Then, I began to hear them more often until it was multiple times a day. I recall one day where I heard them as I was speaking to my mother. We were conversing about visiting my grandmother in Denver when I heard them creeping behind me. I attempted to disregard them as calmly as I could, but I couldn't fool Mother. That night, I overheard my parents talking about my sudden personality change. They were planning to send me to a therapist. I didn't blame them.

At that point I had heard the steps 27 times, 27 horrifying times. You would expect for each time to get less and less frightful, but it didn't. It grew eerier each time. Each time, it got longer. Each time it gets closer. They were haunting me, taunting me. It began to make me feel as if though I were going insane. I was petrified. Sometimes I'd run for miles. Some days, I'd run until my lungs felt as if though they're going to collapse inside my body. In the beginning, I would hear the footsteps sparingly, but as time went on, they began to terrorize me more until they were an almost normal part of my life.

I was afraid as I would turn every corner. I was terror-stricken when I would turn my lights off at night to go to sleep. I was anxious when I would go into the bathroom to shower. I would tremble when I was alone. I never knew when they'd be back. It could be back at any given moment. I was terrified, and I couldn't live my life like that anymore. I wasn't sure how much longer I could handle it. I was bound to explode at any moment. It had to come to an end. I didn't know what to do anymore.

I could hardly eat. I could hardly sleep. I couldn't carry on normal social interactions with anyone anymore. The footsteps filled my mind. I couldn't think of anything else. It had to stop. If the footsteps didn't kill me themselves, they'd be the death of me. I needed help, but no one would believe me. No one would understand. Everyone already thought I was going crazy. They'd never experienced anything like that. I needed help, but from whom? Who would believe me? Who would even know what to do?

I decided to saunter over to the local chapel after school one day to obtain holy water. The chapel contains beautiful rose-stained glass windows, Victorian architecture, and dark maple pews. Although it's quaint, it's beauty is timeless. It looked like one of those chapels that you would see in old black and white movies. It had a pointed roof and a small tower with a crucifix perched gracefully on top of it. I went into the chapel and headed to the altar where the crimson white holy water fountain lay. I had seen enough horror films to know that evil spirits despise holy water. Surely, blessing myself and my room would help keep the spirit away from me for a while.

I knelt there carefully gathering some of the holy water into my bottle. I wouldn't consider myself a very religious person. As a matter of fact, that was the first time I'd stepped into a church in years. I know that the only thing that could save me from this negativity is God. I had faith in myself and in the higher power to get me through this. The spirit could only drag me down if I let it. For the first time in a long time, I felt safe inside the church.

I left the chapel, ready to head home with newfound hope. It was breezy outside that day. The trees no longer had any leaves on them. I remember the sun lightly warming my body as I walked down the street. Tranquility enveloped me, and I was content. After walking for a few moments, I began to hear footsteps behind me. I tried to brush it off, convincing myself that it was just another person trying to get to a destination like myself. For once, I was not absolutely horrified by the sound of footsteps. I continued strolling home, but after five minutes, the footsteps were still in the background. I was overridden with the sudden feeling that it surely must be them again. I continued to try to walk at my normal pace, reminding myself that no matter how fast I moved, they still always keep up with me.

My actions and image as of late, since the footsteps had appeared, had been making me act and appear aloof. I decided I didn't want to draw any more attention to myself. It was broad daylight, and the last thing I needed was the town folk seeing me run away from an invisible monster. Scared, I continued to walk casually, but then for the first time the footsteps began gaining speed on their own. I was not moving any quicker, but it seemed as if though that time they weren't just trying to scare me. They wanted to get me.

I began picking up my pace. Yet, they were walking faster and faster yet again. I began to jog lightly. I could hear them scurrying rapidly on my heels as I burst into a full sprint. They were directly behind me at that point. I must have been in fingers reach of my attacker. Out of breath and trembling in terror, I sprinted directly into my home. I ran towards the kitchen, hoping my mom would be in there fixing dinner. Surely, the footsteps would leave me alone if my mom or someone else was in my home. I got to the kitchen, but tragically, I found no one in there. The house was silent.

The footsteps had stopped running and were now approaching me, strutting slowly behind me. I ran to the end of the room and got against the wall. I was so close to the taupe kitchen wall that I was nearly hugging it. Tears were now streaming down my scorching hot face. My body was shaking. I was horrified, racking my brain thinking about what was bound to happen at any given moment. Terrified and with the last ounce of my bravery, I turned around slowly. For the first time, I saw who had been haunting me. She had pale alabaster skin, hazel green eyes, long messy dark brown hair. Her face was beautiful, serene, yet somehow twisted in a very sinister way. Her lips were curled slightly on one end. She began to open her mouth as if though she was about to say something, but her vocal chords emitted no noise.

To my shock the person standing before me was no one other than myself. My body was now becoming numbingly cold as sweat rushed down my face. My head spun like an overactive merry-go-round, and everything began to fade into a dark abyss. My knees began to give out slowly underneath me. I no longer had the strength to keep myself standing. My breathing became stagnant and weak as my decrepit body plummeted to the ground. I had gone mad.

About the Author

Alma Munguia is an up and coming author from the Los Angeles area, taking up creative writing on her free time. Alma enjoys reading various styles of literature. She takes pleasure in writing in her spare time, whether it's jotting down ideologies, poems, or even creating future excerpts for novels. When she's not creatively writing, she is producing special effects horror makeup. Her writing style has been influenced vastly by horror and the psychological mind. She hopes to write novels in the horror and thriller genres in the very near future.

UNEXPECTED OUTCOME

Miguel Obregon

"I know it seems hard sometimes, but remember one thing.
Through every dark night, there's a bright day after that.
So, no matter how hard it gets, stick your chest out,
keep ya head up.... and handle it."

Tupac Shakur

Mickey was someone that never saw himself wanting kids. He couldn't picture himself in a family setting, He knew kids could drastically change the way people live their lives. They were annoying, and they fight all the time over what seemed to be nothing at all. But, Mickey ended up having a kid, then another, which made him realize kids were actually great. They could make someone take different perspectives on things and could turn any bad situation into a good one. He had his first kid at nineteen, which posed difficulties that kept him from certain goals in life, but he soon realized there were a lot of good that came from of being a young father. He learned to change his day-to-day routine to cater to his kids' schedule, which keeps a young father very busy. All in all, he wouldn't have it any other way.

Mickey was a roughneck kid who started off living in a pretty nice area in the western United States, but he soon moved to a neighborhood where gangs and violence were a way of life for many people. He began living at Mom's house with Mom, a kind heart, and Dad, a rolling stone of sorts, who were influenced by the 60's, drugs, and partying. Mom and Dad split up when he was 10. Dad went to jail for partying too much, but he was soon back on his feet, somewhat. By the time his dad was back working, Mickey was well on his way to a life of crime and trouble as he was the middle of four kids at a house with just mom, two older brothers, and a younger sister.

At thirteen, Mickey's mom couldn't handle him anymore, so she sent him away to stay with his dad who had moved down the street to a much rougher neighborhood. Mickey was quickly tested on the street. People would ask him where he was from, trying to instill fear and intimidation, but he stayed strong never backing down. Suddenly, he found himself in a place where kids had the same issues he had with getting into trouble and not having the necessities at home.

Living with his dad, things were hard, no money, food, or water at times. They did what they could to get by.

One day, Mickey met a young lady, the same age as he, who was visiting some family in his town. Her name was Lucy. They fell for each other pretty fast before Lucy could even go back home. She had gone through some of the same struggles that he had growing up, they had a lot in common. Mickey and Lucy both finished high school in a hurry. He moved out of state to be with her. Soon, they moved in together and found they loved the way things were going. The two would party whenever they wanted, took trips, and lived spontaneously. They got married eventually, and said they would be two forever. They neither wanted nor thought about having kids. The day they returned home from their honeymoon, surprise! Baby number one was on the way, Mickey freaked, and so did Lucy. They pulled themselves together and decided to move forward with their family.

Mickey was infatuated with his new son, Amo. He spent as much time with him as he could, also he tried to beat the odds by staying married. Amo grew up fast, curious about life and eager to find every piece of information in it. He was adventurous, outgoing, and lovable, truly an asset to the family. Just about the time Mickey was getting used to his situation, Lucy hit him with a bombshell. She's pregnant again. That time with a beautiful baby girl named Mae, who seemed to be the exact opposite of their son, very tough and hard to compromise with but was also silly, sweet, and willing to help someone who needed it, at the request of Mom and Dad of course. Mae was the missing piece to their family. Then, with two kids, things were getting crazy around the house, considering both parents worked full time. The kids were constantly fighting, fighting over this toy and that sock. Mickey had to learn how to be a referee, trying to decide which kid was in the right.

As he got used to all the sibling rivalry and the family life, there were times where life got to be too much to deal with and Mickey considered giving up. When life got hard, the kids always knew what to say. They would ask what was wrong with their dad. He would tell them they wouldn't understand money problems. The kids would say something like, "Well, I found a penny today. Maybe you can pay the rent now." He would look up at the kids, give them a big hug, and say, "I love you guys." Mickey realized kids were there to change his perspective on certain things.

The day-to-day routine changed a lot over the years for them. Mickey and Lucy went from doing whatever they wanted, whenever they wanted, to formulating a well-oiled machine that is the daily routine. The first thing in the morning, everybody would get up together, get ready for the day. Mickey would get showered, while Lucy made his lunch. Amo would wake up, while Mae would be in the other shower. Once done, everybody would leave the house. First, Mickey; then, Lucy would take the kids to the bus stop. Then, she would get ready for work, clean the house, and get going. After work, Mickey would pick the kids up from school, pick up Lucy from work, and stop by the store on the way home for items needed. Once home, it was pj's and preparation for the next day.

Never wanting a family, Mickey was sure glad to have ended up with one. His children changed his life in a major way and for the better. Furthermore, all the fighting the kids do, he realized, would never stop. He just needed to find a different way to approach them. Mickey was still amazed that the kids changed his outlook on things. They could make lemonade from lemons. There were pros and cons to being a young father, but he preferred it the way it was for him. He'd rather be young, broke, and there for his kids, than old, rich, and too busy for them.

At the same time, Mickey came to the conclusion that the day-to-day routine he had developed, centered around his kids' schedule, helped him to become a more productive member of society and an excellent role model for his children. He is an unexpected outcome for someone who seemed to be going in the wrong direction in life, heavily influenced by gangs, violence, and negative behavior. Mickey is a great example of the American dream, demonstrating how one can grow up in any kind of environment and overcome stereotypes by working hard and striving for excellence.

About the Author

Miguel Obregon has been through a lot in his life, from living in a broken home, growing up around drugs and alcohol, trouble in the streets, and behavior problems in school. As a result of growing up the way he did, Miguel realized through it all family means the most to him. He is the middle of six kids, two older brothers, two older sisters and a younger one. He has been married to his best friend now for 11 years. They have two kids: Angel, who is 7, and Adrain, who is 10. Miguel wouldn't be who he is today if not for his parents: a mother who is loving, forgiving and always making sure everyone is taken care of before she is; and his father, who had problems of his own, realized having kids in his life means more to him than partying. Miguel also lost a lot of really close friends and family to gang violence and drugs. Because of this, Miguel makes the most out of every day, outdoor activities with his family, staying as humble as possible, and thanking God for having made it this far.

Family's Ghost

Karina Pedraza

"Aiming for a happy soul."

Karina Pedraza

Family always comes first. That's what I've been taught ever since I can remember. It's true though. When you're at your lowest point with nothing to offer, no friend or partner will be there to support you. My family isn't perfect or the biggest, but we are close.

My mom likes to call me Javi, but my actual name is Javier. My dad likes to brush my hair whenever he gets the chance even though I am three inches taller than he and almost twenty years old. I don't mind the annoying nicknames or obnoxious gestures. I feel like I have the responsibility to make my parents happy even if I'm not. I owe them that much.

My parents both work for the police department. I recently graduated high school and work at a local shop on the weekend. And let's not forget, my baby sister Leslie. I call her a baby, but in reality, she's four and the biggest brat alive, almost as big of a brat as her older and oldest sibling, Maryith. If only Leslie had the chance to get to know her before Maryith's disappearance.

The bond between Maryith and me was unbreakable. Like any close siblings, she had my back, and I had hers. We went to the same high school and had mutual friends. She would defend me when rumors occurred. As an older sister and only being 5'3, she sure was intimidating. As for me, I would have her back when she came home late at night drunk or went on dates. It was rare for us to fight. We had our arguments, but for us to yell at each other at the top of our lungs, only occurred once.

Three years ago, on December 15, 2013, was the last time I spoke to her. It was over her not coming home. She was on drugs- on who knows what. Maryith called me at 3am from a phone booth asking me to pick her up. She sold her phone for some booze and drugs. I refused to pick her up and scolded her, telling her to find her own way home and fast or I was not covering for her. But, she never came.

The morning after, my parents asked, and I lied once more. I thought she had slept over at her best friend's house, but later that afternoon, her friend came looking for her. I had to confess to my parents about where Maryith had really gone the night before. A search party was formed, but she was nowhere to be found.

The week before her disappearance, she had stopped wearing makeup, developed baggy eyelids, and sold most of her valuables. She blamed the weather for her odd behavior, but little did I know her real story. The rumors eventually got around about her substance abuse.

We currently live in Seattle, where it's always raining and gloomy outside. We have one of the biggest depression population here, so when something tragic happens to us, it's kind of hard not to feel blue with the weather. It is one of the reasons we are getting away, hopefully to somewhere warm and sunny, like California or Florida. My parents always dreamed of me attending college after high school. To make them proud, as soon as we buy a house, that's the first thing I'll look into. Maryith would've loved to live in California.

Today is the day. It's August 4th, and we're finally leaving this sad town. We're on to a new better life out in Florida. I was accepted into the University of Florida, and I am pretty excited. During high school, I was well-known, had a lot of friends, but no time to have a social life. I had no time for a girlfriend or best friend. I had too much responsibility: homework, babysitting and working a 12-hour shift, during the weekends.

A month has passed, and I instantly became friends with a guy named Jacob at the university, who introduced me to other people whom I now consider friends. I was invited to a massive party on Saturday night. This time around, I plan to make time for my friends, so I accepted.

Saturday night finally came. It was a nice, fresh night which was rare to feel. I probably looked strange because everyone was in sweaters, trying to keep warm, while I wore a short sleeve shirt. As Jacob introduced me to more of his friends from a nearby college, a girl in particular caught my attention. Everyone in the group was conversing and laughing, while she was trying to convince the guy she was clinging onto to leave to another party. She was tan and had medium-length hair with a tattoo I recognized. It was my sister.

I felt an adrenaline rush filled with nothing but anger. My eyes suddenly locked on her and I went charging towards her. All along, my family thought she was kidnapped. We thought she died. My mother suffered from panic attacks and my dad suffered heart break. We all did. Maryith knew I knew, so she fled out the front door to her car. Except, I didn't let her. The rush controlled me more and overpowered my self-control.

I caught up to her, and I immediately yelled at her for an explanation. "I was going crazy over there. I got into too much trouble, I couldn't dig myself out. I wasn't happy. Nothing good would've been made out of me. I'm really sorry," Maryith explained in a whiny, guilty voice, which used to work on me three years ago. But then, it just infuriated me. I would have never imagined the day I wouldn't miss her voice. After a minute of silence, she tried to console me with questions like, "What are you doing here?" "You go to school here?" "Did you come alone?" "Answer me." All I had to say was no in a monotone voice. I left it at that.

I really wanted to tell my parents about seeing her, but I felt as if it was best not to. To think she didn't even leave a letter or note, leaving her family in the dark. I had never come across a ghost before, but she can definitely be described as one.

About the Author

Karina Pedraza was born in Anaheim on March 4, 1998. Karina has two siblings. She is the youngest and the only female. She graduated from Buena Park High school in 2016. She is currently attending Fullerton College and will transfer to Cal State Dominguez Hills. She will major in Human Services and become a youth home coordinator. Her dream is to help adolescents who struggle and have a place to turn to when in need. She has a passionate hope to help others achieve their happiness, so that one day they can look back at their lives and honestly say they are happy with their choices and beat the obstacles in their way.

Driving Tired

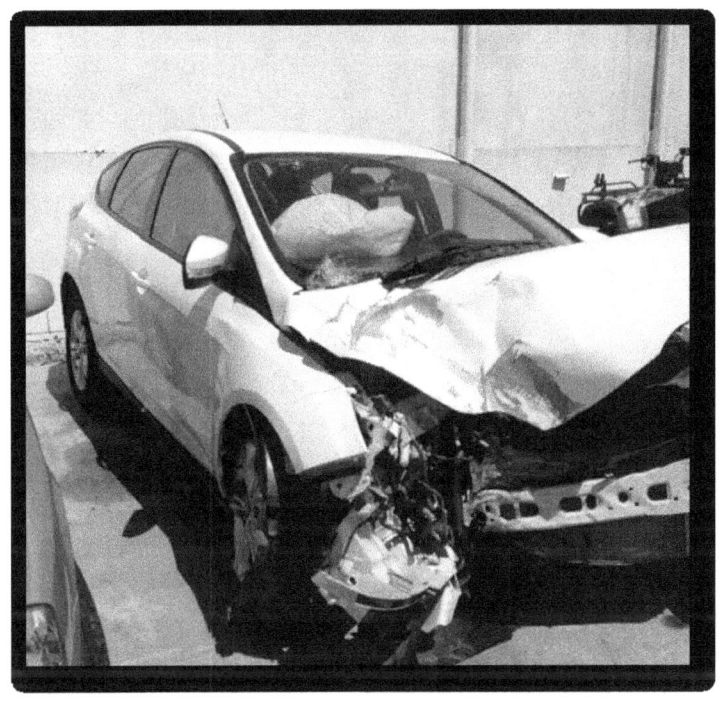

Tyler Rogers

*"That night really made me appreciate life,
and all the little things we take for granted."*

Tyler Rogers
(two days after the accident)

It was the first weekend my friend Andrew and I had off since we got back from our deployment a week ago. It had been a long six months, and we were ready to finally unwind and see where the weekend would take us. Andrew was one of my fellow Marines and a close buddy of mine. We carpooled each week together because we both lived in the same city Orange County, CA, so naturally we became close friends. Andrew was a relatively levelheaded guy and was very friendly to people. We decided we would head to a close friend's house in Long Beach, CA, for a BBQ, stay overnight, and then leave in the morning.

We arrived at my friend David's house around eight o'clock at night. David was a longtime friend of mine. We went to Marina High School together and played on the school soccer team for four years. We arrived to a house packed with people everywhere, from the back patio to every floor in the house. We quickly learned that this wasn't going to be a actual BBQ but a party, which was far from what we were expecting. Andrew told me we should just stay for a couple of hours and then head back early in the morning because there really wouldn't be any room for us to sleep. I agreed with what Andrew said, but I told him the only way I would leave was if he would drive. I was so exhausted from work that week and knew that it would not be smart for me to drive. Andrew agreed, so I told him to let me know when he was ready to leave.

After a couple hours of hanging out with old friends and catching up on what we missed while we were deployed, we both decided to head back home before the exhaustion of being up all day hit us. After saying our goodbyes, we walked out to the car and started our way back home. Normally, it would only take us thirty to forty minutes to get home taking the freeway. But after 11:00pm, it was shut down for construction work. Andrew was forced to take side streets, which added an extra thirty minutes to our trip home. About fifteen minutes into our drive, I fell asleep. That morning, I woke up for work around 3 o'clock, which easily defends my exhaustion. About forty-five minutes later, I woke up and we were in Westminster, only twenty minutes from Andrew's house in Santa Ana. I asked Andrew if he was good, and he simply told me, "Yeah, bro. I'm good. You can keep sleeping." I nodded in assurance and quickly fell back asleep. Little did I know that he wasn't alright and only five minutes from his house he would doze off behind the wheel.

I woke up to a sudden jolt; it was the front passenger tire hitting the curb. The car coasted over a fire hydrant and finally ripped a light pole out of the ground. The initial impact of the collision was so loud. It sounded like a bomb going off. Once the car stopped rolling, I quickly undid my seat belt and opened the passenger side door. I immediately fell to the ground. My back felt like it was on fire and jolts of pain were running up and down my back. Andrew quickly ran over me to realize I was seriously hurt. About thirty seconds after the accident, people came out of their houses, and not soon after that, a police officer arrived. He told everyone to stay back. I had a back injury and any movement could make it far worse. Ten minutes later, I was in an ambulance on my way to the Santa Ana hospital.

Every bump in the road made my pain jolt through my back down to my feet. The paramedic told the driver he needed to slow down, because she could see the pain in my face. As soon as I arrived to the emergency room, I noticed how cold it was and how white everything seemed. The doctors had to cut off all my clothes to help eliminate too much movement due to my back injury. They rushed me to the MRI machine to take scans of my whole back and spine. I was extremely nervous going into that machine. It was so small and I felt like I barley fit into the machine. It was loud and just an unpleasant experience. After the MRI, the nurses took me into my room where I would be staying for the night.

After all of that, it was only seven in the morning, but it felt like I had been up for days. Really, I had only been up for over twenty-four hours. Once my medicine kicked in, I was out for the count. I woke up about six to eight hours later to my mom right by me smiling. She was happy to see her oldest son of four was alright for the most part. Since the morning of the accident, I had not seen my friend Andrew. I was extremely worried about him, so I asked my mom how was he. She told me he was fine and only had a minor bump on his knee. I was so relieved he was okay.

Shortly the doctor came in with the results from my MRI. He was not the friendliest doctor. He was about six feet tall, and he seemed very standoffish. He told me I fractured a bone in my lower spine, and due to the high impact of the accident and me lying in my seat, I slid forward so hard that it compressed my spine. The doctor told me I was very lucky, and that if I would have completely broken that bone, I would have been paralyzed from the waist down. He said that I would have to do months of physical therapy and wear a lower back brace for a few months, but other than that I would be fine. I was relieved to know that I was going to be okay, but I was also full of regret for making an irresponsible decision. That night definitely changed my outlook on life and made me appreciate things I once took for granted.

About the Author

Tyler Rogers was born in Madison, IN. He moved to California when he was seven years old. He joined the Marine Corps in June of 2012 and was honorably discharged in June of 2016. He currently resides in Riverside, CA.

Silence

Joshua Scott

Why won't you speak?
Where I happen to be
Silent
In the trees
Standing cowardly
I can feel your breath
I can feel my death
I want to know you
I want to see
I want to say
Hello

Twenty One Pilots

The sun was eclipsed by the thickness of ominous clouds causing the day to have the same brightness as the void of space. The clouds unleashed water that poured down as if it were a spray of bullets. Meanwhile, in a vast timeworn manor, located in a desolate forest, sat two girls in their early twenties. The storm outside, along with the darkness of the forest, fueled the murderous nightmares of sadistic psychopaths. The need for safe haven from these thoughts was only made dire as a slam echoed off the decaying lumber front door.

(2 Days Prior) {Alarm Sounds} It was just the beginning of fall, and golden maple leaves flooded the ground, as they fell from their oak pedestals. Jessica's short frame of 4'9 was sprawled across her bed like a ragdoll. Jessica hopped out of bed at feats unfeasible of someone of her stature. Jessica's long blonde hair was tangled beyond the repair of her brush. Much like her hair, Jessica contained enough stubbornness to fill someone triple her size. Jessica threw on an arbitrary timeworn black shirt along with faded-out gray sweatpants.

"There is no way I'm going to be late on my first day," shouted Jessica, in such a headstrong voice that it could make a 6'6" male bodybuilder quiver. She had been plagued with that powerful yell for most of her life. No one had been able to fully understand how such a powerful voice could come out of such a petite girl, but that was the norm for Jessica. The constant stares for such an enormous voice broadcasting from such a tiny frame. Jessica burst threw her front door just to greet Tiffany.

Tiffany (Jessica's best friend from what it seems like the womb) was the polar opposite when it came to Jessica in pure physical traits. Tiffany was a giant compared to the fairy-type frame of Jessica. Tiffany was a towering force at 5'10" with long legs like a model with long flowing brunette hair that rolled down the back of her vertebrae. She was dressed in a high riding short skirt and a crop top sporting her favorite artist compared to Jessica's just climbed through dreamland look.

As Tiffany's eyes shot towards the direction Jessica was full on sprinting from, she burst into a full-on laugh. Not the type of laugh Jessica was used to hearing when Tiffany tried to act innocent around the cute guys at school, but a hyena's laugh with which Jessica was even more familiar.

"YOU'RE WEARING THAT?" Tiffany exclaimed through her laughs.

"Well do you see me wearing something else?" Jessica snapped back in her well-known sarcastic tone.

"On our first day of college?" Tiffany said in a sly tone. "You're wearing hobo shek, Jessica" (knowing Tiffany's need to look good at all times expect no less from her best friend)

"Well it's all the rave nowadays," Jessica exclaimed as she buried her face into her phone.

Time seemed to fly as they cruised down the crowded highway towards their esteemed campus. Tiffany was driving as she always did as she liked to give Jessica shit for being unable to reach the gas pedals. Tiffany sported a 2015 Honda in eggshell white, and Jessica's mind always seemed to imagine as if they were a chicken embryo in that damn thing but seemed to push it back to her mind as long as they got to places without cracking. Tiffany had her eyes dead set on the cracked worn down sun bleached highway, while Jessica sat in the passenger seat "Stalking her Ex's Facebook." As they pulled off the bustling highway, their eyes spotted the luxurious campus. The campus had an 1800's Victorian look: It had three main buildings, two of which were above average height, and one building penetrated the sky like a rocket.

They entered the office, Tiffany as always got glances but so did Jessica this time for reason she was led to believe to be different from her friend. "NEXT WEEK!?!?!" exclaimed Jessica her voice echoed with the same power of multiply sirens. The office attendant looked startled but Jessica as usually was unaffected by the increased amount of stares. Tiffany (working as damage control) butt in.

"Sorry for my friend, Miss," she stated with tremendous sincerity. "She thought we started today not next week," Tiffany further explained. "It was just a misunderstanding."

The office attendant still looked unsettled but gained her composure and calmly asked the two girls to leave.

As they entered Tiffany's egg of a car, Tiffany glanced at Jessica. "I have something we can do to kill the rest of the week."

Jessica was intrigued. "I'm listening," she said with a sarcastic tone, as she scrolled through Instagram.

"Let's go to my uncle's manor," explained Tiffany: That was enough to get Jessica's full attention.

"You have an uncle?" said Jessica in a confused tone. "Who has a manor?"

"Isn't that what I just said?" asked Tiffany. "It beats staying at home all week, and we get to relax before classes start," pleaded Tiffany.

"Can't you just go alone?" stated Jessica.

"Well, yeah. But, I want you to come," expressed Tiffany.

"I guess then" said Jessica unenthusiastically.

"Awesome! Just be ready in two days, and I'll pick you up and take you to the manor," said Tiffany with the most energy.

(Two Days later) The business of the city faded, as they got further and further down the highway. The buildings were replaced by towering redwoods and imposing pines, the sound of constant horns and reves of engines were replaced by the dead silence of the forest. The nicely paved road gradually turned into a less unkempt path until it was entirely dirt. The two girls were inside Tiffany's egg of a vehicle. Anyone who had seen her car knew it wasn't meant for off-roading, but that did not faze Tiffany. Jessica, on the other hand, was terrified. Unsure if it was the constant crashing sound the car made or the complete emptiness of the forest along with the deep black colds that filled the sky that fueled her nightmarish thoughts.

"It's going to rain!" Jessica stated with anger in her voice.

"There it is," Tiffany said blatantly, ignoring Jessica's bitching. The manor being called old was an understatement; it seemed to have been around even before Jessica and Tiffany were even a thought in the universe. As they pulled up in the embryo mobile, they took a second to take in the scenery. As they began to unpack their baggage, they couldn't help but feel as if they were being watched.

"This place is unsettling," exclaimed Jessica. "Can we go back?'

"No," Tiffany said in an angry tone. "We did not drive all this way to go back."

"Fine!" exclaimed Jessica. As they unpacked, someone watched from beyond the old decaying tree line.

(Flash forward to opening paragraph.) The slamming was continuous on the old oak door. It wouldn't hold for long. Jessica and Tiffany only had one room to hide in the manor. (The manor only being able to hold 1 normal and 2 max was a problem.) The master bedroom was the only room, other than the living room. As they rushed into the room, a crash of lighting corresponded with the door, as it flew off the hinges. He was in. "WHAT ARE WE GOING TO DO?" screamed Tiffany, as she pushed her weight up against the door. "I DON'T KNOW," yelled Jessica. A sudden epiphany filled Jessica. "I CAN USE MY PHONE." She pulled it out of her pocket and dialed 911. "Someone help us," she pleaded. "There is someone in the house," but Jessica was greeted by the most violent sound she had ever heard…. Silence.

About the Author

Joshua Scott enjoys writing along with skateboarding. He aspires to major in English and hopefully excel as an English teacher. Joshua also is a diehard baseball fan and enjoys spending time with friends and family. #JDF16

The Wedding Day

Juliana Slaven

"Love won't be tampered with, love won't go away.
Push it to one side, and it creeps to the other."

Louise Erdrich

The day was like any other day. The air was cold and crisp. The sun was shining just how September weather is supposed to be. But that day, in particular, was the big day for Alana. It was finally her wedding day. That day, she woke up with joy and felt as if she were going to explode. She was finally marrying the true love of her life, Matt.

Once Alana got up, she went over to her friend Mary's house where her sister, mom, and aunts were there to help her get ready for the big day. Her bridesmaids dressed in the lilac purple dresses she had chosen out for them. She then did her hair and makeup and felt like a beautiful princess. Her hair was pinned up into a flowered bun; her makeup was light and natural with her favorite pink lipstick. She put on her grandmother's diamond sparkling necklace that shined brighter than a star.

All that was left was to put on her dress. She put out her white dress and everyone in the room gasped at how beautiful she looked. It wasn't your ordinary wedding dress. The dress was a soft white, with lace detailing and crystals in the front. Then, she put on her white simple heels, and completed her look with a white lace veil. Everyone looked at Alana as if she had just stepped out of a bridal magazine. By the time she was done getting ready, it was time to head over to the ceremony. She walked out of the house and into the black limo with all her friends and family. They were finally on their way.

On the way there, all Alana could think about was how Matt was going to react when he saw her and if he was feeling as excited as she was right then. All she hoped was that everything went well and that nothing ruined the best day of her life.

She arrived at the ceremony, which was in a small little chapel that overlooked some mountains. Inside the chapel were lights on each side and flowers on each pew with a white sparkling chandelier right in the middle and a white carpet that would lead her to the alter.

It was finally time. The doors of the chapel opened. She could hear the orchestra playing "Here Comes the Bride." Alana's bridesmaids went in one by one, followed by the flower girl, who dropped rose petals on the floor. Alana was overcome with happiness when she saw Matt in his black and white tux, with his blonde hair neatly combed and his blue eyes locked on her. She couldn't stop smiling. Her father took her hand, and both of them walked down the white carpet with red rose petals, as both families stood with smiles on their faces. As Alana was walking down, she could see Matt and his excited face smiling at her. She could tell that he was in awe of how beautiful she looked in her wedding gown.

She couldn't stop thinking that she was finally going to spend the rest of her life with her one true love. She and her father reached the alter, as her father then gave her away to Matt. She could tell that Matt was a bit nervous. He had been sweating. The droplets were running down his face. They finally held hands and exchanged loving vows, both of them saying how they would spend their whole lives together through sickness and in health. Matt then took the ring to put on Alana's finger, and as he did, he collapsed to the floor. Everyone gasped and screamed at what had just happened.

Frantically, Alana dropped to the floor to see if Matt was okay, but he was not responding. She screamed in terror for someone to call 911. Everyone ran around franticly as Alana lay on the floor with Matt's limp body crying. After about fifteen minutes, the paramedics arrived. They rushed in and worked on Matt. They told Alana they found a weak pulse and needed to take him to the hospital if they wanted to save his life. So, the paramedics get the gurney and loaded him into the ambulance. Alana jumped in not wanting to leave Matt's side.

As they rushed to the hospital, Alana felt like she was in a dream, pinching herself hoping that she could wake up from the terrible nightmare. The thought of losing Matt gave her a sickening feeling in the pit of her stomach. The paramedics took Matt out and rushed him inside, as Alana held his cold hand. Running down the hallway by Matt's side, she slowly let go of his hand, hoping that was not the last time she would see him. A nurse in blue scrubs with long black hair saw Alana in her wedding gown. Alana, in such disbelief, was guided by the nurse to a waiting room with the green chairs. Alone and scared, Alana sat in her dirty wedding dress, filled with tears and makeup.

Her worst nightmare came to reality when a surgeon in black scrubs and a white coat approached her. Alana stood hoping for good news, even though she could tell by the doctor's face something was wrong. The doctor explained to her that they did everything they could to save Matt's life, but his heart was too weak to stand the surgery. The reasoning for his collapse was a massive heart attack. Alana's face turned white as she heard the news, and she fell to her knees screaming in pain and sorrow. The day that was supposed to be the happiest day of her life turned out to be the worst.

The love of her life was then gone forever. After Matt's death, Alana tried to go out to live a normal life without Matt and even tried to find love again. Every time she did, she realized no one could replace Matt because Matt was the love of her life. She always felt empty as if something was missing. Years and years passed, and Alana held onto Matt and never let go of him. Alana now being as old as she is with her gray hair and wrinkled skin lay in a cold white hospital bed sick with death creeping up behind her is at peace. With only the couple of hours she has left and taking her last breath, Alana now has the certainty of being reunited with her one true love, Matt.

About the Author

Juliana Slaven was born in Anaheim, California, in 1997. She then grew up in the city of Placentia and currently lives in Fullerton. In her early years, she attended private school then attended public school through half of elementary and throughout high school. Throughout her academic years, she received many awards. She graduated high school with a Val-Tech diploma. She now attends Fullerton College, focusing on receiving her AA and transferring to a four-year university. Juliana is a dedicated, hardworking, and a family-oriented person.

Good Friends

Rodrigo Timis

"The ever-changing light sheds its words."

Rodrigo Timis

On the outskirts of Krasnoyarsk, a quiet town in the Siberian Taiga, a house shimmers with warm light in the complete darkness of the early morning. The light barely penetrates through the cracks of the wooden door, which is covered in a heap of snow due to the violent winds last night. Inside the house, Danil stirs in the pot and deeply relishes the strong smell of freshly ground coffee blending with the boiling water. Soon enough, the smell fills the entire house and slowly sparks his wife's olfactory sense; with a lazy movement, she tries to open her eyes and stretch. From the shelter of the warm blanket, her arms slowly emerge into the cold air and her crystal-blue eyes swiftly open – in a heartbeat, she is up on her bare feet, touching the brisk oak floor. Next to the bedroom, Danil and Anastasia's kids sleep like bears during hibernation. Anastasia quickly puts her slippers on and rushes through the icy corridor into the kitchen, where Danil calmly sips his hot coffee, while sitting next to the fireplace.

While staring outside the frozen window at the city lights slowly turning bright, he encounters Anastasia's desirous eyes; in no time, he gives up his cozy chair and takes her a mug of refreshing coffee with some cream on top. She sips delightedly and looks at him with affection. They start to converse in order to catch up with each other, because last night, Anastasia was already sleeping when Danil arrived home from work. It was a hard week at work for Danil, more people than often needed to have their cars serviced.

Now, it is Saturday and his weekend just had a great start. Half an hour into their conversation, Lev and Sofya show up in their pajamas all sleepy and demanding hugs; Danil and Anastasia kindly welcome the two early birds and serve them with some hot chocolate and marshmallows. It doesn't take too long for the kids to recover their vivacity and start playing and enjoying the morning with their parents.

After a prolonged breakfast, the ashy sun slightly peeks over the gray clouds, shedding a few faint beams of light over the kitchen window. Noticing this, Danil starts packing his supplies and tools in order to head out and get some firewood. The forest is nearby, so he decides to take his dog along for a ride too. Danil hops into the carriage with a wide smile on his face and waves goodbye to his wife and children.

Just like on any other regular day, Danil steers his horse on the path to the forest and greets a few of his neighbors, who are already exiting the woods with piles of lumber in their carriages. As he progresses deeper within the woods, the only present noises are the stamping of the snow, the squeaking of the rusty wheels, and the rustling of the leaves. Surprised by the unusual silence, he begins vividly whistling to cheer up the mood. A few miles in, he settles for some sturdy trees that seem suitable for his powers. Swinging the sharp ax back and forth into the thick trunk for quite some minutes, the heavy sweat starts to pour down his forehead and his back gets wet under the leather winter coat. Nothing unusual, he takes a sip of water and returns to cutting even more vividly than before; the sweat rolls off his nose right into the frigid snow, leaving deep marks around the trunk. Some time passes by, and the great tree falls down under the ultimate swing of his ax.

Pleased by the results of his hard work, Danil makes himself comfortable on the bark and grabs some food. Of course, his trustworthy friend should get a generous portion too, but he is nowhere to be found. Danil listens closely and distinguishes a faint barking sound in the distance. Mildly disturbed, he waits patiently for his dog to return, holding the food in one hand and the ax in the other. As the noise becomes louder, the horse gets increasingly irritated. He shakes his head violently, stamps his feet against the ground, and tries to turn around. Now, having a better sight of his dog, Danil understands why he is rushing; following his pet, an immense brown bear charges at full speed, brutally ripping apart everything in her way. Instinct kicks in, and Danil tightly grips the ax waiting for the beast to approach. But, after a second thought, he turns his eyes to the carriage, yet it's too late – the horse is already galloping in the distance far away from his immediate reach.

In a split of a second, he turns his head just to see the monstrous creature six feet away, viciously raising her heavy palm with the claws prominently sticking out. With a pitiful move, Danil tries to block the strike with his ax. But the creature does not even notice the human's strive to survive, and her powerful bony claws enter Danil's shoulder and continue their way implacably all across the chest, leaving a deep laceration. Entirely shocked at the initial experience, his body sends enormous amounts of adrenaline throughout every cell. Unfortunately, the energy rush does not make up for the sectioned muscle. So despite the fact that his hand is still clenched onto the ax, he is incapable of using it. Imprisoned in his own body, Danil has no other choice but to collapse before the animal and pray for mercy. But the beast knows no God.

Shortly after the helpless man crashes down and tries to protect his vital organs, the bear unforgivingly slashes his back open with three savage blows, leaving his coat drenched in scarlet red. At that moment, all of Danil's memories roll in front of his eyes like a motion picture. Seeing his master pinned to the ground, the dog flees urgently, too. With a reserved movement, Danil shifts his sight towards his last friend sprinting through the sparse vegetation. He gathers his last powers to hold his breath and feign death.

The bear's yellow eyes blatantly scan for any signs of life; any potential threat to her cubs will be permanently removed. The bear slowly smells every inch of the mortal and relentlessly inserts her stained fangs deep into his left hip. A sound radiates – the pelvis is slit by a profound fissure. Feeling the injury, Danil abruptly clenches his teeth into the frozen dirt and uncontrollably jerks the muscles in his body. Despite the pain continually jolting his nerves, he desperately tries to remain silent – but the effort is too great, and his body is suddenly immobilized. Everything turns black before his eyes, and he loses consciousness. Inhaling one last time, the melting snow permeating Danil's hair, the beast steps heavily over his body and struts back to the cave. As the spiritless sun continues its arch over the impenetrable blanket of leaden clouds, the blood continues to drain, seizing every speck of chalky snow, enclosing the body.

During a moment of awareness, a warm touch – a soothing caress of gentle hands lingering over his pale cheeks and heavy lips meeting his forehead – sparks his senses. His inner essence slowly infiltrates through his bones, flesh, veins, and soon enough he regains enough strength to open his eyes and produce a fragile smile. Savoring this moment, Anastasia tenderly embraces his rejuvenating body and pours tears of joy over his frail chest. Right next to the bed – noticing the events – Sofia and Lev quit playing with their plush toys and rush to show affection to their beloved father. Concurrently, their dog – the one who previously alerted everyone about Danil's encounter and led them to the scene – lays his harsh paws over the edge of the pillow and lightly licks Danil's cheek with the rough pores of his tongue. Certainly, Danil's recovery will be lengthy and arduous, but his family is happier than ever to see him breathing, and they are ready to offer him all the support that is necessary.

About the Author

An avid programmer, runner, and nature-lover, Rodrigo never quit his passion for writing literature. As of eight, he wrote his first short story entitled "Melting Mr. Snow." Later, after his teacher unfairly accused him of plagiarizing one of the stories he composed for an assignment, Rodrigo knew writing could be an intriguing new field to explore, so he participated in a few Romanian Language and Literature Olympics. Nevertheless, when he started programming, much of the spare time initially dedicated for writing or hiking (or sometimes both) had to be spent learning new algorithms, etc. So, his involvement with such literate/sport activities decreased. Fortunately, since he arrived in the U.S., his focus temporarily shifted towards a wider field expertise, so he found the opportunity to explore a little more of the wonders of literature and California. With a refreshing restart, writing might start to gain a larger role in his life.

CANCER

Everardo Valenzuela

Learn to forgive, learn to let go, and learn to appreciate life.
I know you're not alone up there in heaven, like we are not alone
down here on earth. I know you have met up with my mom in
heaven, and I know you two are finally in peace.
You two have left me, Mario, and Jackie in great hands.
Now, I wish you two nothing but the best in your new lives.
Rest in peace,
Mom & Dad

One early morning, at approximately five o'clock, as I was sleeping, I heard a loud knock on my window. To my surprise, it was my father asking me to open the door to my house. Once I opened the door, my father asked if I could take him to the hospital. At that very moment, I knew something was wrong, because my dad was not the type of person to go to the hospital.

My dad was very strong for his age, always optimistic, and the kindest guy you could ever meet. My dad was the type of person who even though he didn't know you, he would greet you with a very positive attitude and make you feel good about yourself. He had to be the strongest man I knew. He was a widowed man with three kids, including myself. So, when he asked me to take him to the hospital due to a sharp pain in the stomach area, I was worried.

Once we got to the Anaheim Regional Memorial Hospital, I started getting flashbacks to when I would be in the emergency room a lot as a kid. As kid, I would constantly be in different hospitals due to my mom's sickness. Even though we were there for my dad's pain, all I pictured was me sitting in the emergency room full of people with pain, kids crying because of how hurt they were, and even some people that were cut open really badly, just bleeding everywhere.

Once they checked my dad into his own room, all sorts of doctors were constantly coming in and out checking on his pain and running different tests. In my eyes, all I saw was my dad being poked with needle after needle and him just in pain. It hurt me a lot seeing my father in pain. I felt like every needle, every medicine, every MRI, and every CT scan was being done to me. All the pain my dad was having, I felt it myself. I couldn't stand seeing my dad hurt. It was killing me inside. I had already lost my mother at the age of fourteen. I couldn't see myself losing my father also at a young age.

Once all tests came back in, my family was in the room with my dad. As the doctor came walking in, with a very serious face, my family was feeling extremely nervous. The doctor announced my dad had liver cancer due to all the drinking he did.

As the first couple of months went by, my dad was living life as if nothing was wrong even though he knew he had cancer. One thing I noticed and that played a part in my dad's sickness was that he was still constantly drinking. I was so confused as to why in the world would he continue drinking, if drinking was the reason he got liver cancer. My family was constantly trying to help him out by taking him out to places and even we, his own children, would beg him to stop drinking. The bad thing was that the more we would help him, the more he would drink. It seemed like my dad's pride wouldn't allow him to change his lifestyle just because he had cancer. He was too prideful to let go of his daily lifestyle to start a new lifestyle that would benefit him.

My dad's cancer meant constant hospital visits. When the doctors would examine him, they would all ask him the same question, and that question was, "Have you been drinking?" In my mind, I'd answer the question saying, *Yes, he has been drinking.* But, my dad at times would lie and say, "No, I have not been drinking." Every time my dad would reply with that answer, I would look at him with an upset face. In my mind, I always wondered, *Why lie? How is lying going to make you better with your sickness?*

As the doctors ran more tests on my father, they were able to see that he was still drinking. Once the doctors noticed he was still drinking, they gave him more bad news. The doctors told him, "If you keep drinking, you are only going to have two more years to live. Drinking isn't helping you get better. As a matter of a fact, it is killing you." Once I heard that statement, I felt as if I got the air knocked out of my body. My dad, being so optimistic, replied to him saying, "Thank you, Doctor. I understand." All I could think of was, *Hopefully, he can change for the better now.*

From my point of view, if a doctor tells a person, "Stop drinking or you have will have a high chance of passing away," any human being would stop drinking. However, to my surprise, my dad just wouldn't stop the bad habits of his. At times, I felt like he loved his beer more than his own kids. Why would anyone endanger his/her life by doing something that could kill him/her and hurt the loved ones around him/her?

As time went by, my dad started feeling worse and worse by the day. As the doctors predicted, the alcohol was killing him from the inside. My dad went from living a so-called perfect life then had to live with constant hospital check-ins and nothing but pain. All the doctors could do then was stop the pain and send him home. Even though my dad was constantly living with pain, he was still living with that positive mindset full of happiness and very optimism, at least I thought so. Deep down inside, I knew my dad was seeing life differently by the way he would act. He went from walking with a happy face and a positive attitude to walking slowly with a neutral face.

Finally, what the doctors had predicted from the beginning happened. My dad passed away. As the day got closer to my dad's funeral, all I could feel was my heart pounding faster, my adrenaline rushing through my veins, and my head was full of flashbacks. As I entered the big white church and walked down the walkway that led to my dad's casket, all I remembered was walking down the same walkway that led to my mom's casket.

Once I got to my dad's casket, I saw him peacefully lying down. All I thought about were the memories we had created, but the memories brought pain, pain brought anger, anger brought sadness, sadness brought depression, and with that same depression came suicidal thoughts. With all my emotions being locked away in my head, it made my heart rush through every beat.

Enjoy what you have while you still have it. I lost so much in a matter of no time. I lost my mom at the age of fourteen and lost my dad at the age of twenty. My dad would say he drank because it was a way for him to get rid of his bad thoughts, but truth be told, it was the road to his own deathbed. Every time I would see my dad, it was like I was seeing a ghost of his former self. Knowing what was waiting for him at the end of all the drinking he did and watching him not care was devastating.

My whole life I lived with pain in my heart, feeling like good can come in the future but only worse would come. I'm at the point of life where I wish I can just knock at heaven's gates just so I can know how it is to live in a stress-free life. The life I'm living is worse than staying at the devil's place. I've been through so much in life at a young age that it has me living an angry life and also has me feeling like I'm at my lowest and never at my highest potential.

Before my dad passed away, I would ask God for one request every night before bed. That request was to let me dream of my mom, but now I ask God for a different request every night. That request is to be reunited with my parents in my dreams, so I can hold them once again.

About the Author

Everardo Valenzuela was born on February 14, 1995. He was born to Hilda Reynoso and Mario Valenzuela. Everardo has a brother named Mario and a sister Jakelyn. Growing up, he was really into sports. He would spend most of his time playing baseball. Going into high school, at the age of fourteen, Everardo's mom passed away. Everardo graduated high school, and once he did, his dad found out he had cancer. After two years, his dad passed away due to his cancer. Now, Everardo is student at Fullerton Community College.

The Ghost Girl

Joselyn Violante

"Faith is not believing that God can.
It is knowing that God will."

Ben Stan

In a small village, in Central America, there lived a young girl and her mother. They were a happy family. The mother was a teacher who gave lectures on architecture and English. The girl was only three years old and loved her mother very much. The little girl was beautifully named Bella. She had pigtails all the time as well as always wearing cute little tutus. As a single parent, the mother, Daisy, was always caring for her daughter and spoiling her every chance she got. One day, while sitting in the living room enjoying a summer evening, the mother heard her daughter talking to herself as if she were playing with someone else. The mother thought to herself that no one was with her daughter nor did she have a playmate over. The mother went up to the second floor of their home into her daughter's bedroom.

When she got to Bella's room, the mother asked, "Sweetheart, to whom are you talking?"

"Mommy, it's Prin," replied the girl. As the mother looked around, there was no one to be found. Bella then ran downstairs and acted as if nothing ever happened.

Granted, it was rather odd that all of a sudden Bella leaned off the subject, but the mother decided not to acknowledge it and moved on. The next day, as Bella and Daisy were getting dressed for their day out. In the bedroom, Bella started staring off to the corner of the room.

Her mother noticed and immediately asked, "Bella, what are you looking at?"

"Nothing, Mommy. It's just Prin," said Bella. The mother at that point was beginning to feel frightened and worried about why her daughter continued to see such a figure. She asked Bella if "Prin" was pretty or ugly, and she responded ugly. She asked if Prin ever touched her, and Bella told her, "Yes, on my shoulder and wrist." Now, more fearful than before, she knew her daughter was seeing and talking to a being not of this world.

Daisy asked Bella to try not to talk to "Prin" anymore because she was worried and scared that the being was a bad one that could harm her daughter. But each time Bella seemed to bring up "Prin" or even acknowledge that she was even there, it was when she passed a room across the hall before she went upstairs to her bedroom. Daisy, out of fear and desperation, began to talk to the being to see what she wanted with her daughter. She began to ask who it was, why she was connecting with her daughter who was young, and she even asked if she needed help to guide her to the light. Of course, the being said nothing back to her, but Daisy knew she would have a sign from it soon.

The next day, Daisy called her mother to ask for advice about what to do. Daisy's family was known to be superstitious, so she figured one of her family members could help her with the situation. Daisy's mother began listening to everything that was going on and thought to herself for a while.

"Daisy this could be either one of two things. Either your daughter has the ability to talk to the dead and communicate with them to help them fulfill what they need to pass through the light, or the being is something bad and eventually is going to hurt your daughter. Either way, she is much too young to go through such things and pass through all of this."

For a while, Daisy thought if her daughter had that ability then what being in their home was trying to communicate with her or would need that type of help. Then, it sort of came to her that before they moved to their current home, two old ladies lived there for almost 60 years. Daisy knew they loved their home, and they would have done anything to protect it.

The old ladies, as she recalled, were also very superstitious about everything as well. Daisy thought that maybe one of them was just trying to cross through to the other side but couldn't because she couldn't let go of her home. And, maybe her daughter was the only way to help, but of course, she was much too young. As Daisy began to explain everything to her mother, Daisy's mother began to give her simple instructions on what to do to help free the being and leave her daughter alone. She told her to go to the nearest church first and talk to the Father to see what he had to say about the matter. The priest told her to go buy white flowers and a white candle. They were to be put on any altar at home that she had and to light the candle.

Daisy's mother told her when she had everything set up, with faith, to tell the being that was bugging her daughter to let her be because Bella was too young to help her in the way she needed. She said to tell the being that if it really needed the help, to please follow the light from the candle and cross to the other side into a better place. Daisy, with a little more relief, did everything her mother told her. She bought the flowers, the candle and continued to always look out for Bella as any mother would. Once Daisy followed all the instructions, she felt a sort of relief and a sense of much needed comfort for Bella as she was going to be safe in the hands of God and her loving mother.

After a few days, it was as if nothing happened. It all became a blur throughout the rest of her days. They lived a long happy life with so many joys and never had a problem with supernatural beings ever again. It's amazing how life could be with faith and how great something as little as what Daisy did to help her daughter and protect her in so many ways.

About the Author

From the age of seven, Joselyn has always wanted to someday be a writer. After her future career as a medical physician and surgeon, she hopes to write medical books and stories that she encountered through her job and life. As the oldest of three in her family, she wants to show her brothers that anything is possible no matter one's age. No matter what goes on in life, one must always keep going. She dedicates all of her work to her parents, most of all.

Fear

Wendy Waite

"Fear reminds us that some things are worth overcoming."

Anonymous

Do you recall the last time you wanted to do something, but intense fear got in your way? This is a story about my experience abroad. My husband travels all over the world quite frequently for his job. He has been to Australia, Belgium, Tokyo, just to name a few. One day, he called to tell me he was planning a trip to France. He then proceeded to ask me if I wanted to go with him. I was so excited that I almost dropped the phone. I emphatically said, "YES!" He continued to say that if I could find someone to care for our children, he would make the travel arrangements. I agreed, then realized I only had two weeks to get ready. I had a ton of things to do before that time. Needless to say, those two weeks flew by super-fast.

After twenty-two hours of traveling, we finally arrived at the hotel in a town called Clermont-Ferrand. It is located about four hours south of Paris. Although it was almost morning, we collapsed into bed and slept extremely well, the kind of sleep that makes you drool and have crazy dreams. I awoke late that afternoon. I was experiencing intense jet lag, which I had never had before. My husband had already left for work. As I walked over to the window and peered out, I could see we were situated near a busy intersection. I saw many people walking up and down the street, and some were walking their dogs. I saw people riding bicycles, which I found a bit odd because the weather was so cold outside that it had started snowing. I also watched trains as they went by every ten minutes or so. It was all so interesting to watch. I felt as though I could sit there forever. I could remain curled up with the warm comforter and hot cocoa and be completely entertained.

It didn't take long for me to realize the magnitude of the situation, and I became completely overwhelmed. I realized that for the first time in my life I was completely alone. Before I left home, I told my sisters and my friends that I would get pictures of the places that I visited. I couldn't go home and tell everyone that I stayed in the hotel all week long. My thoughts started to spiral out of control. I thought to myself, "What if I am kidnapped?" Have you ever seen the movie *Taken*, with Liam Neeson? That's a pretty scary movie where the girl gets kidnapped and her father hunts down the bad guys. Only in my case, it would be my husband, and he wouldn't even know where to look for me. Another problem is that my cell phone only works in the United States. *What if I get lost? I thought. Calling for help is out of the question. In addition to all of this, the only French that I know is from my high school days and only consists of about three basic phrases. How will I ask for help?*

While I was sitting there feeling very small, I decided to make a list of the things that I wanted to do while there in France. I knew I wanted to explore the local cathedrals. From the books I had read, they have a rich history. I wanted to spend money. I had approximately two hundred euro in my pocket that I could spend however I wished. I also wanted to talk to a stranger. I know that this goal sounds a little weird, but I wanted to have a conversation with someone local.

When the next morning came, I was ready to head outside to find a fabric shop that I saw on the internet. I had money in my pocket, my passport, and a map of the area. After walking for about an hour, I started to feel anxious. The signage in town was not very good. I had a hard time understanding where I was. As I walked down a cobblestone street, I noticed the fog had rolled in. The gently falling snow started to turn into a hard rain. My heart started to beat faster and faster. I couldn't hear anything but the thud, thud, thudding of my heart. I felt as though "Jack the Ripper" would jump out at me at any moment. There is no doubt, I was terrified.

I was about to turn around and go back when I saw a fork in the road. I had a choice to make. I looked to the left and just saw an empty street, but when I looked to the right I saw a sign that told me I had found the fabric shop. Eureka! I was so excited! I stepped into the shop and took a deep breath to slow my heart and calm my nerves. The shop owner looked at me with a funny look, but that was understandable. I was a mess. She understood a little English so we were able to communicate pretty well. I ended up spending most of my money in her shop. She helped me to use the metric system when cutting the fabric that I purchased. When I left the fabric shop, I felt emboldened. From that point on, I felt like I could accomplish anything. I felt completely energized. I spent the rest of the week visiting every cathedral that I could walk to. I discovered an amazing cathedral named Notre Dame de l'Assomption. It was made from volcanic rock. This was an absolutely incredible site to see. It had an unbelievable dark gothic appearance that stood out among the red tiled roofs of the surrounding buildings. I also visited a few small clothing shops and purchased delicious chocolates and macaroons. There were many inspiring art galleries. The parks I visited were beautiful, but I was told to visit them again in the spring when the flowers were in bloom.

Taking everything into consideration, that was an opportunity of a lifetime. By putting my fear behind me, I was able to grow as a person and expand the possibilities that surround my life. I cannot wait to return, and next time, I would like to take my children. To sum it all up, don't let your fears hold you back. Let them be your guide.

About the Author

Wendy Waite is an easy-going and creative writer. She is fond of sharing her life experiences with people all over the world. She also loves to hear stories from others who have similar interests. She loves everything related to writing since her freshman year at Crafton Hills College. In her everyday life, she enjoys sewing, quilting and scrapbooking. Wendy currently lives in Southern California with her loving husband and two adorable children.

Just a Hobby

Guadalupe Zuniga

"But you, take courage!
Do not let your hands be weak,
for your work shall be rewarded."

2 Chronicles 15:7

Andra pauses in front of her nearly-finished painted canvas. She holds her paintbrush with a slight grip and gives an apathetic stare over her art. *I've been in my bedroom painting for nearly three hours, and this still isn't coming out how I want it to be*, she thought. She has a desire to tear the canvas. She picks it up from the messy easel but quickly realizes she can't because it is her art assignment. Placing it down slowly, she sighs. She has less than twenty-four hours until this assignment is due. Normally, the short time pressures her to work faster, but this time, it doesn't. She loves drawing ever since she can remember and decided for her last year of high school to challenge herself in an advanced placement art class.

As a child, she loved art like anyone her age. Unlike most children, her art seemed to "stand out" from the rest. She received encouragements from her classmates and teachers, who helped build her confidence to try harder. It was the first thing she believed she is good at, and she wanted to get better at it. Andra soon started to take a sketchbook everywhere she went, such as to the playground, to class, and to the restaurant. Every opportunity, when she wasn't doing anything, she would engage in her favorite hobby, especially in her room.

Her room would most likely be mistaken for an art studio with a bed. Her small dark wood bookshelf is filled with sketchbooks, paints, brushes, and five unopened school textbooks in the bottom left corner. Next to her bookshelf is her desk that has permanent paint stains even on her desk chair. The desk is cluttered with all sorts of color pencils, pens, and miscellaneous papers. Those papers might be homework from another class, but she doesn't pay much attention to them. Her paintings are hung all over her walls and sketches are pinned to her bulletin board. She also likes to make small plush animals out of cheap fluffy socks. The animals lay on her grey and orange blankets on the bed.

Andra had just started to take art seriously because of her art class. She liked drawing as a hobby and as a stress reliever. Her art teacher encouraged her talent and convinced her to apply for an art college to pursue an art career. She loved the idea at first mainly because she doesn't know what to do after high school. Being an average grade student, maybe even close to being below average, she doesn't have a passion to study anything. Although she hasn't told her mother about her choice, she even applied for art scholarships all over the country but hasn't heard from any of them.

She stops sulking over her art now and checks her phone to see the time. "She should be here now," she mumbles. It's a holiday on a Monday, but her mother had to go to work. The sound of a garage opening startled Andra, and she quickly ran downstairs. Her mother exhaustingly, holding two grocery bags, manages to open the door somehow and close the door with her foot as she enters the house.

"Ma!" Andra shouts. She grabs both bags from her mother's hands.

"Why are you still wearing your pajamas at three in the afternoon!" her mother asks.

"I was busy doing homework," Andra replies. "Ma, can I talk to you? I think I finally decided on a college I want to go to." Her mother walks to the kitchen and Andra follows.

"Oh really? That's great. Place the bags up here." Andra nods and sets the bags down on the kitchen counter. Her mother continues, "So what UC or Cal State did you decide?" She begins to put some groceries away in the fridge.

Andra smiles and laughs nervously, "Actually, I decided to apply to an art college." Her mother stops for a second then proceeds back to the groceries.

"I thought it was just a hobby like you told me."

"I want to give it a try."

Her mother closes the fridge slowly and explains, "Give it a try? Colleges are not cheap you know. Why don't you choose a different school and study something that will guarantee a job after you graduate?"

Andra knew she would say that, and she understood why. Her mother migrated to a different country in order to get a better job to support her family. She gave up her life for her children and only wants the best for them. She doesn't want them to deal with not having enough money like she did. But art is the only thing Andra has a passion to study even though she is starting to lose that passion because of her difficult art assignments.

Andra hugs her mom's arm and decides to plead, "You know I'm really interested in art. This won't be a waste of time or money."

Her mother brushes off Andra's arms from her hand. "If I had enough money you know I would send you off to any school you wanted."

Andra admits defeat, and without saying a word, she helps her mother with the groceries. The silence is unbearable for the both of them. Andra's mother stops and lets her daughter finish while she gets the mail from her purse.

As she looks through the mail, she sees one is for Andra. "Here this one is for you." Her mother says while she passes the envelope. Andra recognizes the school logo and opens it quickly. "Why are in such a hurry? What it is?" Her mother is talking, but Andra isn't pay attention because she is reading the letter.

She gasps and says, "Mom, I got accepted. I got accepted to the art school I applied for and they are offering me a full ride!" Her mother covers her mouth in surprise and rushes over next to Andra to read the letter. Andra's eyes begin to water, and quietly she says, "Can I still not go?"

Her mother hugs her and thinks for a moment. "You really want to go?" Andra nods and her mother continues, "Okay, give it your best! I guess it really isn't just a hobby!"

About the Author

Guadalupe Zuniga is a first-year college student at College of the Desert. Later, she will transfer to pursue a teaching credential. Some of her interests include painting, crafting, and playing the piano. Guadalupe was raised in Indio, California and lives there currently. She is a second-generation citizen who plans to pursue whatever future is in front of her.

About the Editor

Dr. Cassundra White-Elliott resides in California with her family, where as an English/Education professor she teaches at various community colleges and universities.

When writing, she writes with the direction of the Holy Spirit, in an effort to share with God's people all that He has for them.

In addition to teaching and writing, Dr. White-Elliott also serves as an evangelistic teacher. She is the founder of International Women's Commission, a ministry that serves the needs of the entire person, by attending to healing the mind, body, soul, and spirit.

Dr. White-Elliott holds a Ph.D. in Education, a Master's in English Composition, and a Bachelor's in Education.

Dr. White-Elliott is also the founder of CLF Publishing, LLC. For publishing, go online to www.clfpublishing.org.

Gift of Salvation
for Non-Believers

"For all have sinned, and come short of the glory of God."
(Romans 3:23)

This section was written especially for non-believers, those who have not accepted the gift of salvation. The gift of salvation saves souls from eternal damnation and is a free gift offered by God himself.

John 3:16-18 says, *"For God so loved the world, that he gave his only begotten Son, that whosoever believeth in him should not perish, but have everlasting life. For God sent not his Son into the world to condemn the world; but that the world through him might be saved. He that believeth on him is not condemned: but he that believeth not is condemned already, because he hath not believed in the name of the only begotten Son of God."*

This section of scripture tells us God's purpose for giving His son Jesus to the world. The world was in a bad condition. The world was overwrought with sin; the people were living for fleshly desires rather than for God's desires.

As a result of the world's conditions, God decided He would offer the perfect sacrifice that would save the world from being a place where people were lost and had no hope. He decided that His own son could stand in proxy for the sin-filled world, taking all sin upon Himself.

So Jesus came, born of a virgin, to save this dying world. He walked on this earth for 33 ½ years, doing the work of His

Heavenly Father. At the appointed time, He died by way of crucifixion upon a cross at Calvary, on Golgatha's hill. He shed his blood and died for you and for me. Because His blood was pure, it paid the penalty for all unrighteousness and gave those who believe in Him direct access to His father's throne.

Scripture tells us in Matthew 27:51 that the veil of the temple was ripped in two from top to bottom, at the moment that Jesus' spirit left His body. As a result of the veil's removal, we are no longer required to have a high priest make intercession for us. We, as the children of the Most High God, are able to approach the throne God for ourselves, and Jesus sits on the right hand of the Father making intercession for us.

But what is even more miraculous than God offering His own son as the perfect sacrifice was the fact that when Jesus was placed in grave clothes and placed in a tomb, He only remained there until the third day. God would not have it that His son would remain in the heart of the earth forever. In order for people to believe in the awesome power of God and His dear son Jesus, a miracle had to be performed. So, on the third day, after Jesus died on the cross, He was resurrected, demonstrating the omnipotence of God. This very act was the act that would cause people to believe in a god that reigns supreme and holds the power of the universe in His very hands, a god that could save them from themselves.

Today, if you are an unbeliever, you can change your destiny. You can change where you will spend your eternity. Our Heavenly Father gives us the freedom of choice about how we want to live our life here on earth and how we want to spend eternity. In Deuteronomy 30:19, God boldly declares, "*I call heaven and earth to record this day against you, that I have set before you life and death, blessing and cursing: therefore choose life, that both thou and thy seed may live."*

So, dear friend what choice will you make today? Will you spend your eternity with the Creator or will you suffer Hell's eternal flames? Again, the choice is yours. Just as the men aboard the ship who were with Jonah became believers, you too can make a choice to accept the only one and true living God as your god.

If after reading the above passages, you have decided that you want to spend your eternity in Heaven with God, the creator, and His son Jesus, and the Holy Spirit, read through what has affectionately come to be known as the Roman's Road. This is the road to salvation. As you read through the scriptures that comprise the Roman's Road, you will also read the explanation for each scripture so you will have clarity about what you are reading and confessing.

The Roman's Road to Salvation

The road to salvation begins with Romans 3:23 which declares, *"For all have sinned, and come short of the glory of God."* This scripture explains that everyone has come short of God's glory and needs redemption. Then Romans 6:23a states, *"For the wages of sin is death."* Here, we learn that the consequence of living a life of sin is death. Everyone will experience physical death as a result of the sin committed in the garden of Eden, but those who commit themselves to a life of sin will suffer eternal damnation in the lake of fire (Rev. 19).

Continue with the rest of verse 6:23 that says, *"but the gift of God is eternal life through Jesus Christ our Lord."* There is an alternative to suffering eternal damnation. We can accept the gift of salvation by accepting Jesus as our personal lord and savior. Then, Romans 5:8 says, *"But God commendeth his love toward us, in that, while we were yet sinners, Christ died for us."* We are able to receive the gift of salvation because Christ came to earth and shed His blood for us on the cross.

Continue to Romans 10: 9-10 which says, *"That if thou shalt confess with thy mouth the Lord Jesus, and shalt believe in thine heart that God hath raised him from the dead, thou shalt be saved. For with the heart man believeth unto righteousness; and with the mouth confession is made unto salvation."* If we confess with our mouths that Jesus is the son of God, that he came and died for our sins, and that God raised Him from the dead, we will receive salvation.

Finish with Romans 10:13, which states, *"For whosoever shall call upon the name of the Lord shall be saved."* Call upon the name of God by saying these words, **"Lord Jesus, come into my heart and save me Lord. I believe that you are the Son of God who came and died on the cross for my sins. I believe that you rose from the grave. I also believe that you now sit in heaven on the right side of the Father, making intersession for me. I accept you as my Lord and my Savior.**"

Now that you have confessed with your mouth that Jesus is the son of God and that He died for our sins and rose from the grave, **YOU ARE NOW SAVED!!!!** You will spend your eternity in heaven.

The next step is very important- you must find a Bible-based church that teaches the word of God and confesses the

Lord Jesus Christ to be the son of God. Don't delay. Do this immediately. Do not leave yourself open to the enemy. Get connected with the saints of the Most High God and keep yourself covered with the unspotted blood of the lamb.

Here is my prayer for you.

Father God,

I thank you for the opportunity to minister your word to the unsaved, the unchurched, and the uncommitted. Father God, I pray now for the souls who have just received the gift of salvation. Lord Father, they have opened their hearts to you, and I know that you have received them into your kingdom and written their names in the Book of Life. Father God, I pray that you will touch their lives and show yourself mightily before them. Let their eyes be opened by the scales falling off, allowing them to see clearly.

Father God, I even pray for the backslider, those who have turned away from you after receiving the gift of salvation. You said in your word that you desire that none would perish. So Lord, I send your word to them right now praying that they would confess the iniquity in their heart, repent, and turn from their evil ways, so that they may receive a life of abundance. You said in your word in Matthew Chapter 14, that every knee shall bow before you and every tongue will confess that Jesus is Lord.

Father God, I pray now that we all come under subjection to your word and that we will humbly submit our lives to you. I ask all these things in the name of my Lord and Savior Jesus Christ.

Amen, Amen, Amen!!!!

I will continue to pray for your success in your walk with God. Remember, this spiritual walk that you are about to embark on will not be an easy walk, but remember, the race is not given to the swift but to those who endure to the end.

Be blessed with heaven's best. I love you!

The Mosaic II

Edited by *Dr. C. White-Elliott*

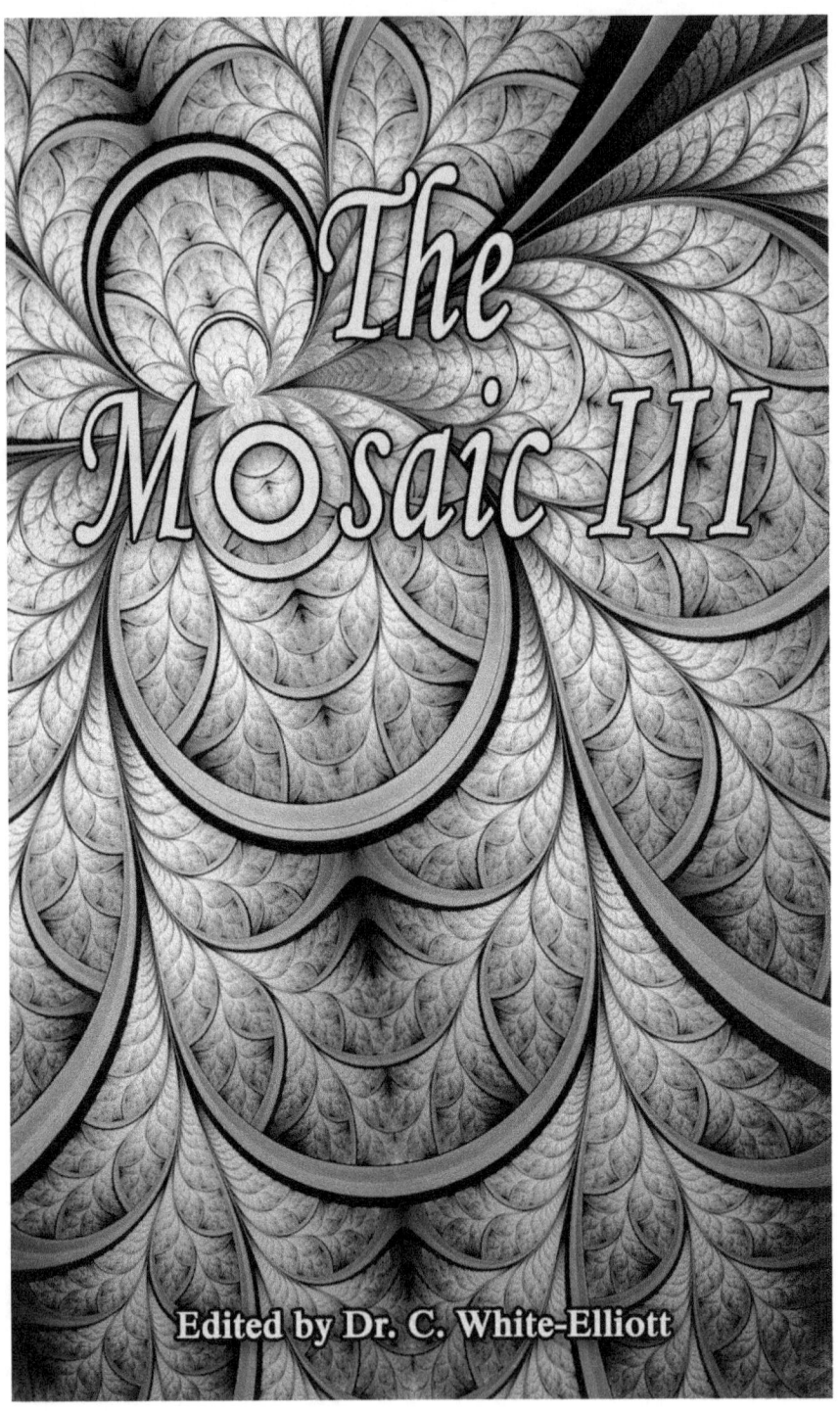

Edited by *Dr. C. White-Elliott*

A Mother's Heart II

Edited by Dr. Cassundra White-Elliott

www.ingramcontent.com/pod-product-compliance
Lightning Source LLC
Chambersburg PA
CBHW050400030726
47503CB00006B/1956